5 Dirty Taboo Lesbian Short Erotica Stories Frist Time Naughty Hardcore Hot and Wild Bundle with Kinky Experience

Steamy Erotic Adult Fiction Collection, Volume 1

APRYL ROW

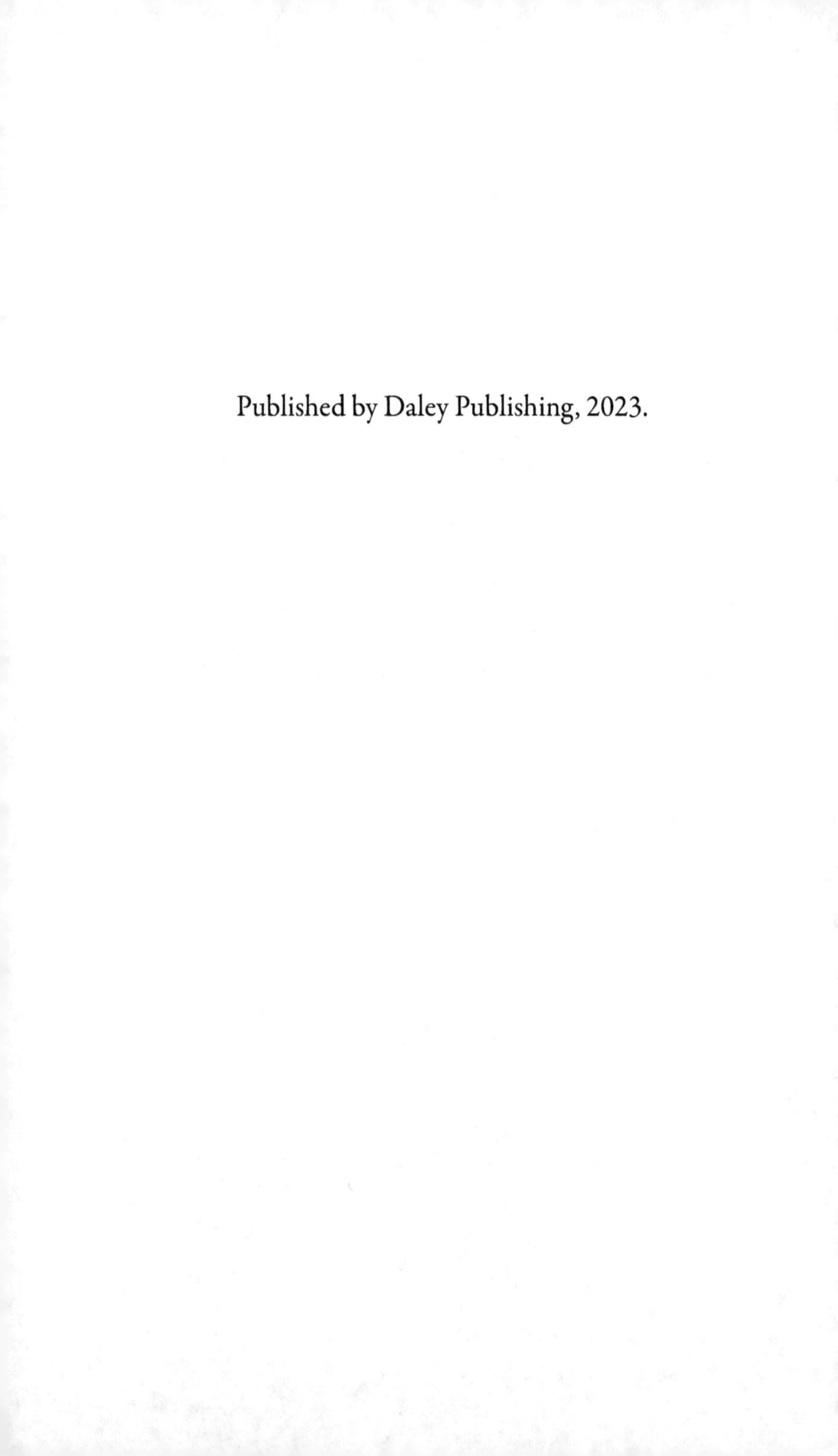

Published by Daley Publishing, 2023.

This is a work of fiction. Similarities to real people, places, or events are entirely coincidental.

5 DIRTY TABOO LESBIAN SHORT EROTICA STORIES FRIST TIME NAUGHTY HARDCORE HOT AND WILD BUNDLE WITH KINKY EXPERIENCE

First edition. March 21, 2023.

Copyright © 2023 APRYL ROW.

Written by APRYL ROW.

Table of Contents

5 Dirty Taboo Lesbian Short Erotica Stories

Frist Time Naughty Hardcore Hot and Wild Bundle with Kinky Experience

Steamy Erotic Adult Fiction Collection
Apryl Row

~

All characters in this book have no existence outside the imagination of the author and have no relation whatsoever to anyone bearing the same name or names. They are not even distantly inspired by any individual known or unknown to the author, and all incidents are pure inventions of fiction.

The Art of Kissing

Table of Content

Chapter 1

"Poppy, for the last time, I'm not going."

Poppy was an expert at ignoring her roommate and best friend, Millie, whenever she felt the other girl was talking nonsense. Like now.

"Shut your tits up, you'll thank me for this later when you're having the best sex of your life," Poppy rolled her eyes, still rummaging around her best friend's closet. She made a triumphant sound, turning around with a simple black dress with a deep V neckline. "Wear this and your boot, let's go."

Millie closed her book with a thump, adjusting the glasses sliding down her nose. "You know I'm studying for a reason, right? Not all of us are naturally brilliant and can afford to mess around while still getting good grades."

Poppy sighed. "One night out isn't going to leave a dent on your oh-so-precious GPA, Millicent."

Oh, Millie hated being called that, and Poppy knew it too.

With a snarl, she snatched the dress up and stripped out of her pajamas. "Fine! Look in the drawer, my medicated contacts are in there."

"Yes!" Poppy cheered, scampering over to the desk drawer. "I get to have a hot girl on my arm this time!"

Millie didn't deign to respond, already brushing her hair and searching for her pink lipstick.

The music was so loud, it made her sick. And they hadn't even gotten in the house yet. Worse still, there were some guys passed out on the lawn.

"What time did you say this party started again?" Millie had to shout for Poppy to hear, even though they were literally holding hands.

"10 o'clock, why?" Poppy yelled back.

It was only 10:30 and there were unconscious bodies outside. Great. Millie steeled her nerves, following Poppy inside.

She knew everyone. Literally every single person wanted to say hi to Poppy and by default, the hot friend handing off her arm. Millie could swear it took them ten minutes, just to get from the foyer to the living room proper.

"That's Trent, he's the host," Poppy pointed at a guy sticking his tongue down some other guy's throat. That was fun.

"That one's Jessica. She thinks she's 'that girl' but—"

Millie wasn't listening anymore. There was a girl standing by the window. She looked like Millie felt — wanting to be anywhere but here.

She also looked smoking hot, in denim shorts and a long-sleeved top that had a heart cut just above her chest.

Millie nudged Poppy, trying to point discretely. "Who's that one?"

"Heart top?" Poppy squinted. "That's Eliza. She's in Film, and she doesn't really talk much." She looked down at her best friend, heels making her 3 inches taller. "Ouu, you like what you see, huh?"

"Shut up!" Millie hissed, shoving the other girl.

That's when Eliza looked in their direction, as if summoned. All the air left Millie's body in a rush. Those were the prettiest brown eyes she'd ever seen in her life!

She licked her lips, turning away as her face warmed. Poppy knew what that meant, and she knew exactly what to do about it.

"Stay right there," she told her best friend, steering her towards the only couch someone wasn't making out on. "Don't take anything from anybody and if someone touches you, poke them in the eye. I'll be right back."

Millie couldn't help but crack a smile. She couldn't have asked for a better best friend, honestly. "I'm not 12, I can handle myself."

"Yeah, but you're short enough to look the part," Poppy said before trouncing off.

Millie's mouth fell open. "We're the same height, you cheater!"

Poppy only lifted her middle finger behind her back.

Millie huffed, turning to the side. Only to find Eliza watching her, mouth curved into a smile. Oh fuck, she had dimples. That was Millie's one weakness.

She waved weakly, not to seem creepy. Eliza waved back, and the other girl resisted the urge to melt into a puddle.

The music abruptly went down, and the twenty something people in the living room looked over at the speakers to see what was going on. Trent's grin was almost brighter than the lights.

"Alright, party people!" He yelled for absolutely no reason, since Playboi song was practically a whisper now. "Let's get on with the party games."

Everyone shuffled closer and Millie found Poppy in the crowd, sticking close to her. Poppy's smile looked wicked and Millie suddenly had a bad feeling about this game.

"We're playing Spin the bottle," said Trent, with a shit eating grin. The groans from the crowd over how boring that sounded only seemed to spur him on. "Oh, sorry, I meant spin the person."

Now everyone was curious. It's Poppy who explained the rules, using Millie as a test subject. "We'll pick any of you and slap a blindfold on," she did just that, tying a bandana over her roommate's eyes. "And you have to lift one arm and point. I'll spin you around, and whoever your finger points to has to make out with you while the blindfold is still on."

There were some interested hums in the crowd, some looking Millie up and down like a snack they wanted to devour.

The blindfolded girl grabbed her friend's hand. "I don't remember agreeing to this, Pop Tart," she whispered with urgency.

"You'll be fine, babe," Poppy grinned, even though her friend couldn't see her. "Trust me."

Before Millie could say anything else, Poppy raised her arm and she was spinning. She was really glad she hadn't eaten anything before coming. The last thing she wanted was to puke on someone's shoes. Or in their mouth.

Was she really considering going through with this game? Yes, she was.

Millie came to a staggered halt, and she had barely gotten her bearings when someone grabbed her face and kissed her. She gasped into the kiss, moving her arm to encircle their waist — it was a woman, thank God. And she was such a good kisser, too.

When the woman pulled away, she was left gasping for air as she yanked the bandana off. Eliza smiled down at her, and licked her lips.

"You taste good," the other woman said.

"That was the hottest thing I've ever seen in my life," Poppy whispered behind her. Millie could barely form words.

It took Eliza pointedly clearing her throat before she remembered to let go. "Thank you, um. You're a great kisser," she said, barely aware of the crowd as it dispersed around them.

They were moving a little further into the living room to play some more. Millie could hardly care less.

"You think so?" Eliza hummed, smirking at Millie's hurried nod. "Then may I kiss you again? I'm sorry I didn't ask before."

Millie's brain short-circuited, just a little bit, before she nodded again.

Eliza gently cupped the back of her head, leaned down and kissed her.

The rest of the party was a blur.

Chapter 2

Once more Millie found herself in front of an empty portrait.

She sighed and buried her face in her hands. Maybe Poppy was right, and she did need to go out and get inspired. Sitting here wasn't going to push her anywhere. She kept finding things to distract herself with, and if she wasn't focused on something, then her mind tended to drift to that night and how she really, really wanted to sit on Eliza 's pretty face.

She had touched herself to the thought of it three times already, and it's barely been a week. Why on earth didn't she take Eliza 's number again? Because she was dumb, that's why.

Before walking out of her apartment, Millie picked up her messenger bag from beside her couch, the one that carried her sketchbook and drawing utensils.

Hours later it was already sunset and Millie had yet to find one thing to draw. She'd passed by everything from giggling children playing on colorful toys in the park to a couple on a bench kissing passionately under the glowing, fiery expanse of the setting sun.

Nothing caught her attention.

No matter how much she wanted to deny it, Millie was afraid that Eliza had become her quick fix for inspiration, and the tugging in her gut wasn't going to quit until she saw her again and squeezed a painting out of her.

Millie leaned up against the side of a restaurant and pulled out her sketchbook and a pencil, flipping the book open and taking out her phone. She dialed Poppy's number and held the phone between her shoulder and ear as her hand remained poised over her book.

Three rings and, "Hey Millie, what's up?"

"Hey Pop Tart, listen, I need a favor."

"Sure, shoot."

Millie rolled her shoulder and tapped the tip of her pencil against her book, a passive expression on her face. "I need you to tell me where Eliza lives."

"Are you sure you don't want her number first? Just showing up where she lives would be kinda weird."

"Yeah, well, maybe I'll get inspired if I get laid? I don't know, I'm not sure of anything anymore."

"I'm... I'm just gonna give you the number, okay?" Poppy paused for a moment before sputtering, "Wh-What even makes you think I have her address?!"

Millie sighed and tilted her chin up. "Poppy, I've known you since we were 8. You've had forty-two crushes, twenty-six hook ups, seven real relationships, and always did a background search on guys you were super interested in, even when their answer was clearly 'no.'"

There was a long stretch of silence, and then a flick up at the corner of Millie's lips as Poppy grumbled Eliza 's phone number and address to her and her pencil scratched across the page.

...

Night had fallen then, the moon full and glaring white as Millie looked up in awe and knocks on the door.

Eliza 's family home wasn't exactly a mansion, but compared to her own dinky little dorm, it might as well be fucking Disney World, minus the magic and general awesome.

The door opened and at first glance, Millie thought it was Eliza who'd answered, but as she looked closer, she noticed the differences. This woman was taller and had shorter hair, and was a lot more fit looking than the other woman. "Uh... hi, I'm looking for Eliza?"

Fit woman stared at Millie and snorted. "Hey, sis," she called, "there's another little fangirl here to see you."

Millie jerked back, her face going red. "Hey hey! I'm not a fangirl!"

Eliza 's husky voice was heard in the background, "Tell her to fuck off."

Fit woman continued to stare at Millie. "Are you sure? This one's slightly attractive."

"Slightly?!" Millie gasped, scandalized.

"Wait, I know that voice."

Millie watched as Eliza pushed the taller woman out of the doorway. Her eyes flickered over Eliza.

She was dressed in light blue PJ pants with little strawberries printed on them, and a thin, short-sleeved, white undershirt. There was also a pair of thick, black-rimmed glasses sitting on her nose and her feet were bare.

Millie couldn't help but wonder how the hell Eliza managed to still look good while sporting the I'm-a-nerd-who-just-got-out-of-bed look.

Eliza looked her up and down and crosses her arms, a smirk playing on her lips. "Kind of hoped you'd call, princess, but I guess this works too."

"This is Millie? Ha, I take back what I said about your tastes, sis."

"Carol," Eliza growled in warning while one of Millie's eyebrows quirked up.

Carol waved a dismissive hand at her sister and looked down at Millie. "Do me a favor and tell your roommate that unless she intends to back up her barking with bites, I have no interest."

Millie made a face. "Ugh," she stepped closer to Eliza as Carol flicked her hair and walked away. " Eliza, can I talk to you?"

Eliza 's brow furrowed. "About what?"

"Just, please?"

"It's the middle of the night, princess—"

"Please not the name calling," Millie whined. It was doing things to her, and she needed to be focused for this conversation.

Eliza 's eyes narrowed as her hand slid up the doorframe. "I believe there's a magic word people say when they ask—"

"I think I need you," Millie blurted, a bit desperate, but mostly out of frustration.

Eliza stiffened slightly. "...S'cuse me?"

Millie stepped back and shuffled her feet uncomfortably, looking away from Eliza. "Can we please just... come outside?" She turned and walked away, and after a moment, let out a little sigh of relief as she heard the door close and footfalls trail behind her.

Millie plopped down on the grass of Eliza's front lawn, while Eliza gracefully lowered herself and crossed her legs. She lets out an amused snort, "This isn't necessary, you know. If you had said the magic word, I probably would have let you inside."

Millie was picking at blades of grass, her knees up against her chest. "Nah, I'd rather be out here." She chuckled, "Your house kinda intimidates me anyway."

"Hm..."

Millie bit her lip and scratched the back of her head, then looked up at Eliza and smiled. "So, uh... sup?"

Eliza squinted at her, amusement wavering. "'Sup'? You dragged me out here; I can't be looked at to strike up a conversation."

Millie exhaled heavily and rubbed her hands on her knees. "Okay look, I'll be straight with you. I'm an artist – ah, aspiring, still in school. And I have this final project –"

"What does this have to do with me?" Eliza interrupted.

"If you'd let me finish, God. So, I've been really stuck for a while, you know, art block? Nothing was working, but then I keep going back to that night when you kissed me silly, yeah? And when I got home, I was totally inspired by the... um... feelings, and painted something a lot better than the crap I've been doing lately." She looked up to see if Eliza was still listening to her or had gotten fed up with her rambling and quietly snuck away.

She breathed softly at seeing that she was still there. "What I'm trying to say is... I like you. In fact, you're pretty much the most beautiful woman I've ever seen, and apparently..." She observed Eliza with artistic eyes. It made her mouth go dry to see how her face looked almost porcelain under the moonlight, how it brought out these reddish tints in the dark mass of her hair, which at the moment was messy and loose and so wonderfully disorganized. Her gaze fell lower, to the tight cling of Eliza 's shirt, outlining every smooth curve of her lean and fucking perfect body.

She could have just asked for Eliza 's Instagram handle or something. Someone as pretty as her would definitely have one. But there was something about her — and not just the fact that she wanted to sleep with her — that made Millie want to see her again.

"You inspire me," Millie murmured, unable to look away from Eliza. "I mean damn, just looking at you right now makes me wanna draw you."

Eliza was hoping to God that the darkness was hiding the flush that has risen to her face, rather than the moonlight highlighting it. "...I see," she said, although she didn't really. She just wasn't quite sure how to respond to such a confession.

The tension in the atmosphere was so thick, so palpable, that the thought of it being cramped into a word like "awkward" was nothing short of laughable.

Millie coughed, startling Eliza. "So uh, why don't you tell me about yourself?"

"You first," Eliza replied sharply.

"Oh, uh, all right... like I said, Senior at our school. Um, I guess you already know my name, my favorite food is spaghetti of any kind, and I live in an apartment across town –"

"You don't live with your parents?"

Millie flinched. She'd quietly hoped Eliza wouldn't pick out that particular detail. "They died a couple of years ago in a car crash. I was living with my Godfather and his wife until I turned eighteen and moved out with inheritance money."

"Oh..." Eliza looked off to the side and closed her eyes, a light red on her cheeks, clearly uncomfortable. "I didn't mean —"

"Don't apologize or anything, it's stupid when people do that, like it's their fault or something. You didn't know, it's cool." She pointed to Eliza, "But now it's your turn."

"Tch, there's not much to say beyond what you see in front of you."

"Pft, s'not what I heard."

Eliza raised a fine brow. "Oh really? And what exactly did you hear?"

Millie's legs fell apart so they were crossed, her fingers wrapping around her ankles. "Is it true that your dad had to shut down his company 'cuz he was outing other competitors? And that your sister killed a guy who tried to blackmail her?"

Rumors were big in Cal U, okay? Sue her.

Eliza's lip curled, making a face that clearly showed she has no idea what Millie was talking about. "Where the hell did you hear that?"

Millie flushed and shrugged, making Eliza chuckle. "I suppose when idiots gather, they would spew idiotic things to a princess's delicate hearing. No, my father sold his company because my mother wanted a life away from all the business, where we could be a 'real family.' The name Fjord was thought of from the country my mom grew up so... also her idea."

Millie smiled at her. "Yeah, I think that makes more sense."

A little puff of air burst from Eliza's lips as she stretched her legs out and leaned back on her hands. "Yes, princess, check your sources next time."

They both laughed, slowly but surely chipping away at the tension as they settled into a comfortable air.

"That second part," Eliza continued, "I wouldn't put it past my sister to kill someone, but if she has, I doubt it was for our dad's sake." She let her head fall back with a frown, digging her nails into the earth. "Your friend is loud, by the way."

"Haha, Poppy? Yeah, she's really into your sister, apparently."

Wouldn't shut up about it all the while Millie was pining helplessly.

"Mhm,"

Millie allowed her attention to hang on Eliza, enraptured as she watched her lift her head back up and bring up a slim hand to cover a loud yawn. The action made the little space between her eyebrows wrinkle, causing her glasses to tilt. She looked so normal like this, Millie thought. So not like the sex demon she'd been dreaming of.

"Hey, Eliza?" She murmured.

Eliza closed her mouth and lowered her hand, cocking her head as she looked at Millie with a drowsy expression. "Hm?"

"Would you mind if I drew you? Just your face."

Eliza blinked and shrugged. "I guess not."

Within a beat, Millie had scrambled through her bag and whipped out her sketchbook and a mechanical pencil. She opened to a blank page and clicked her lead out, glancing once at Eliza before resting the pad on her thigh and drawing the general outline of Eliza's face with light, quick lines.

Eliza watched Millie's arm jerk around for a few minutes before growing bored and finding her eyes drifting away, aimlessly running over the green expanse of her lawn.

It was a relaxed silence they sat in, outlined by the soft scratching of the pencil, until Millie suddenly said, "You've got a really nice face."

Eliza looked at her and Millie's face went beet red. Obviously she hadn't intended to say that out loud. "Ah – ah I mean, structure! You know, for drawing..."

Eliza smirked. "Hm, sounds like something you'd say to get in my pants," she teased.

"Come on! It's not like that!" She let out a squawk as Eliza snatched the pad right out of her hands. "HEY!"

Eliza looked over her portrait while holding Millie's face back with one hand. Millie's arms were stretched out toward the sketch, her fingers grabbing at the air. Her face could be seen through the spaces of Eliza's fingers, and she did not look happy.

When Millie tried to lurch forward for her pad, Eliza simply raised a foot and pushed it against Millie's stomach, her knee bent at an awkward angle, and yet, she remained perfectly balanced. "Hm," Eliza mused, "this is actually quite impressive, princess. I like it."

Millie stopped flailing, her heart beginning to pound furiously as she smiled at the praise. "Really? You mean it?"

Eliza gave her a look. "Do I seem like the type to fuck around?"

That's what I want, Millie didn't say. She scoffed instead, "Yeah, kinda."

Eliza chuckled and moved back, tossing the sketch to Millie. "I mean it."

Millie beamed at pad, giddy with happiness. "Hey uh, Eliza."

"Hm?"

"I was wondering if maybe you wanna come over to my place tomorrow? I'm thinking of maybe painting you for my final project."

Eliza's response was the same, she chuckled and shrugged, like it was no big deal. "What do I get out of it?"

"Pft, you get to be a model for the great Millie Raind!" Millie raised her head haughtily. "What more do you need?"

Eliza pushed her glasses up and smirked. "This isn't gonna be one of those cliché things where the artist falls in love with the model, is it?"

Millie's lips fell apart, and she stayed silent before sputtering, "I never said anything about love! And why can't the model fall in love with the artist?"

"I guess that might work too." Eliza stood up, wiping the grass off her pants.

"Wait!" Millie tore out a page and, scribbling her address across it. She held it up to Eliza. "Morning, before ten, you'll be there?"

"Tch," Eliza smiled and closed her fingertips over the opposite end of the paper. "I'll be there."

Chapter 3

Sunday morning Millie made sure to put aside her terrible habit of sleeping in and woke up bright and early at 8 am. Though it hadn't been that difficult to be honest, because she'd spent most of the night twisting and turning in anticipation and unable to sleep due to her excitement at seeing Eliza again.

Millie eagerly tried to make herself presentable. She took a shower, one of those really thorough ones where you just grab that soap and rub your skin raw. She brushed her teeth; finger combed her blonde hair, and dressed in a white tank top and frayed jeans.

Millie quickly set up her paints and easel, already running the colors she'd have to mix in her mind to catch the reddish hue of Eliza 's dark hair, the creamy, pale texture of her skin, the jet black of her eyes – she couldn't remember the last time she was so excited about painting something, let alone someone.

By 10:45, Millie was laughing to herself, thinking God's gift to women must have gotten lost.

By 11:15, Millie was starting to worry. She wondered if Eliza was all right, she didn't seem like the type to say she'd do something and then not do it.

But by noon, Millie was just plain pissed.

She is lying back on her couch, twirling a paintbrush between her fingers with a very nasty scowl on her face.

Millie sighed and threw her paintbrush at the ceiling in anger and more surprisingly, a feeling of hurt. "Damn it"

Eliza wasn't coming.

She was in the kitchen, moping over a bowl of cold soup when there was a knock at the door.

"Come on in, Pop Tart," she called, wondering when her flatmate started knocking in her own home.

"Um... it's me," a familiar husky voice cane as the door opened and closed.

Millie dropped her spoon, rushing to stand. She was caught between a hundred different emotions.

"I'm sorry! I got a work call and I couldn't say no and I finished early, but then I got lost like an idiot and I almost didn't come. Because I thought you'd be so mad, but then I realized I didn't have your number to text you and I can't just stood you up with no explanation." Eliza sucked in a breath. "I'm sorry. It's fine if you don't want to um... paint me anymore."

They were alone, blessedly alone, and she wasn't sure what to do with Eliza now that she was right in front of her. Eliza stood, fidgeting nervously with her watch. They were much closer now that she was standing.

"Oh, I just need you to kiss me," Millie said with a shameless chuckle, before reaching out and grabbing Eliza 's waist, pulling her flush against her. Eliza didn't have a second to comprehend how quickly Millie had moved before Millie's mouth was on hers, her tongue pressing into Eliza's mouth.

Eliza gasped, then pressed her hands against Millie's back, fisting her fingers into her shirt. She stumbled backwards and against the kitchen counter, hissing as her spine met the hard wood. It would bruise, but she couldn't be bothered to care. All she cared about right now was making sure Millie didn't stop kissing her. Millie kissed her way down Eliza's jaw then dragged her lips across the side of Eliza's throat, her tongue pressing into the skin near her ear.

"Is your back, okay?" Millie whispered, hot in Eliza's ear, before she continued kissing her neck. Her teeth bit into Eliza's skin and she gasped again, spurring Millie on.

"Um... yeah, it's fine," Eliza responded. Was it a response? Did she say it out loud? She wasn't sure. Millie's fingers were dancing up her sides, beneath her shirt, and Eliza was far too distracted to make sure she actually answered the question.

Then Millie lifted Eliza with ease, pushing her back onto the counter and moving between her legs. Eliza wrapped them around Millie's back and pulled her in. Millie pressed her lips against Eliza's collarbone, then down the front of her partially opened shirt. She pulled away for a moment, her green eyes looking up at Eliza from beneath the longest eyelashes.

"God, I'm just glad you came in here at all," Millie breathed. Her fingers pressed up Eliza's hips and dipped into the waistband of her jeans. Millie kissed the swell of her breast through her open shirt, then lifted a hand towards Eliza's shirt buttons. "May I?" Eliza nodded, then moved her hand to the front of her shirt to unbutton it. Millie gently swatted her hand away. "Oh no, baby. Let me."

Eliza thought she was on the verge of melting as Millie slowly unbuttoned her shirt, exposing her black bra and toned stomach. Eliza leaned back on her hands, willing herself to meet Millie's eyes. Sucking air between her teeth, Millie moved back a bit, drinking Eliza in. It was like being fucked without being touched. Millie's eyes dragged along every inch of Eliza's skin, setting her on fire. If being looked at by Millie felt this good, she couldn't even imagine how it would feel once she was actually fucking her.

Millie moved back between Eliza's legs and pressed a hand to her sternum, dragging her fingers down her skin, between her breasts. "You... are so beautiful."

Eliza blushed. "Thank you," she said softly.

Millie put a hand on Eliza's cheek. "And that blush. It's too much. I mean, you blush everywhere." She waved a hand towards the flush on Eliza's chest. "It's actually one of the sexiest things I've ever seen." She moved from between Eliza's legs and held a hand out. "Now, as much as I'd like to fuck you on my counter, I don't think it would be the most comfortable for you."

"Oh. Okay, your room then," Eliza mumbled, taking Millie's hand who helped her from the counter.

"Perfect," Millie said with a light laugh. She led Eliza through the living room, Eliza wasn't sure how long it would take them to get to the room, probably an eternity; every few steps, they stopped and kissed passionately, bumping into storage shelves, Millie's desk, a crate of glass bottles that rattled ominously. Their hands wandered further beneath their clothes with each stop, teasing sighs and gasps out of one another. It was maddening.

Chapter 4

Finally, Millie pulled away and pointed towards the corridor. "We need to focus. It's this way." Eliza followed Millie closely and her mind raced. She just needed Millie, now, no more distractions.

Right next to the door, Millie stopped. Eliza bumped into her as Millie turned towards her. Millie stared at her, her lips parted slightly as she breathed heavily, looking torn. A moment later, she mumbled, "Fuck the bed," then pushed Eliza into the wall, her hands already pulling Eliza's shirt from her shoulders, then sliding them down her back and along the curve of Eliza's butt. Eliza drew a deep breath as Millie kissed her way across her collarbones, pressing the strap of Eliza's bra off her shoulder with her nose. "God, I want you now."

Kneeling, Millie unbuttoned Eliza's jeans, pulling them down as best she could. The slightly damp fabric from the rain outside, no doubt stuck to her hips, so she helped, shimmying her way out of them to leave them in a heap on the floor. Millie nuzzled Eliza's stomach, then nipped her hip bone lightly, the sharp but brief pain flashing through Eliza's consciousness.

Her hands rested against Eliza's cool skin, her palms warm and soft, as Eliza stood nervously on the landing. Millie leaned back and drank her in again. Her fingers inched their way up Eliza's thighs, before slipping beneath the edge of her underwear. Eliza gasped as they danced along the elastic, teasing. "I bet you taste as good as you look," Millie murmured, placing a kiss against Eliza through the fabric of her underwear, then she stood and pressed her body against Eliza, only her hand between them.

Eliza braced herself against the wall with a sharp intake of breath, waiting for a touch which didn't come. She opened her eyes to find Millie looking at her, a question on her face.

"Can I touch you?" Millie asked.

Eliza nodded. "Please."

With no further hesitation, Millie slid her hand into Eliza's underwear and pressed her fingers between her legs, and into the wetness that had pooled during the last few hours. Pressing her middle finger against Eliza's most sensitive spots, she hummed with pleasure, then whispered into Eliza's ear, "My specialty."

Eliza whimpered, rolling her hips closer to Millie's hand. Millie reached up with her other hand, bracing it on the wall next to Eliza's head, then leaned down and kissed her neck, her teeth grazing her collarbone as her fingers worked magic between Eliza's legs. For a few maddening minutes, Millie teased Eliza, lightly stroking her, her fingers just pressing inside, but not giving Eliza what she wanted.

Eliza moaned, her head falling back against the wall. The air buzzed, quiet in the dark corridor, the sound of the rain pounding on the pavement outside the only thing that managed to dull the sharp sounds of her breath as it burst from between her parted lips. She was dizzy, her heart racing as Millie bit down on her shoulder. She felt a swirl of heat in her lower belly, coiling tighter and tighter. Something had to give soon and Eliza had the idle thought that it was most likely going to be her self-control.

Then Millie slipped her fingers inside of Eliza and everything went silent.

Millie's fingers curled and Eliza swore she could see stars. Eliza gripped the hand railing, trying to hold herself steady. Was she still breathing? She gasped as Millie did it again, dropping her forehead to Millie's shoulder, another whimper elicited from her mouth as she tried to focus.

Close, Eliza thought to herself. I'm so close.

"Hmm?" Millie asked, her voice raspy near Eliza's ear. "What was that?"

Had she said that out loud? Eliza couldn't find the words to reply, just touched Millie's wrist, pressing down on her hand to spur her on. Eliza felt Millie laugh quietly, then lean back. She dropped her hand from the wall she'd been bracing herself on and gently held Eliza's chin, tilting her head up to look at her. Eliza opened her eyes and met Millie's.

"You're close?" Millie asked. Eliza nodded and Millie smiled. "Good." Then she slid her fingers out of Eliza and took a step back.

Eliza trembled, feeling her legs go weak with need and she leaned against the wall. "Tease," she said, glaring at Millie.

Millie raised her eyebrows. "I never said I played fair."

Without another word and faster than Eliza could process, Millie knelt, pressing Eliza's legs apart, and pulled her underwear down her legs. Then she leaned in and licked her clit, one long and slow pass, and Eliza came undone.

Eliza's hands moved of their own volition, coming to rest on top of Millie's head as she tried to steady herself, her fingers tangling in her braid. She really didn't play fair. Eliza was already falling to pieces, her legs shaking, her breath coming in heady gasps, and yet Millie continued, licking and sucking until Eliza thought she might pass out. She came. Then came again, standing practically naked on the stairs in the back of Millie's bar. She had the vague thought that she should stop pulling Millie's hair but with Millie's tongue darting inside of her, she couldn't quite get her fingers to let go. Instead, she pulled her closer, crying out as she rode the wave of her orgasm.

Millie slowed as Eliza came down, then finally pulled away, her beautiful mouth glistening. She wiped her lips with the back of her hand, a grin cutting across her face. Eliza took a shuddering breath and loosened the grip she had on Millie's hair, untangling her fingers, then leaned back against the wall, trying to slow her heart rate.

Smoothing down her hair, Millie stood. "You've got quite the grip there, blue eyes," she joked. Eliza started to apologize and Millie silenced her with a kiss. She could taste herself, warm and wet on Millie's mouth and moaned. Eliza felt Millie smile against her mouth, then whisper, "I liked it."

"Good," Eliza said, her lips finding Millie's jaw. She kissed her way towards her ear, before biting down on her earlobe. To her extreme pleasure, she heard Millie gasp quietly, then tilt her head to the side, giving Eliza better access to her neck. Eliza sucked the sensitive skin beneath her jaw. She wanted to leave Millie with a memory of the night.

Chapter 5

Millie pulled her closer, one hand pressed against the back of Eliza's head, the other stroking the small of her back.

Then Millie turned, her eyes dark and hungry, and kissed Eliza. Eliza welcomed it, rolling onto her toes to meet Millie's height, her fingers grasping at the back of her shirt. Millie raked her hand into Eliza's hair, lightly tugging at the roots. Eliza groaned into Millie's mouth as her hands danced across Millie's back and shoulders. She slid her arms around Millie as they kissed, guiding her until her legs hit the bed and she fell back onto the mattress, leaning up on her elbows.

Eliza climbed on top of Millie, straddling her, and kissed her deeply. Millie trailed her fingers up the backs of Eliza's thighs and across her butt, inviting her to come closer. Eliza obliged, straightening one leg so she could lay flush against Millie. Her skin met Millie's shirt and she hummed in frustration.

"You're wearing too much," Eliza said in a quiet huff against Millie's throat, sliding her hands up Millie's sides. She heard Millie chuckle before she sat up, taking Eliza with her.

"I think you should do something about that," Millie replied.

Eliza smiled and lifted the hem of Millie's shirt, pulling it up and over her head. She was rewarded with a half-naked Millie, her body warm and delicious in the lamplight as she leaned back on her hands. Millie was braless, a fact that hadn't escaped Eliza's notice. Her tattoo didn't disappoint either. Eliza traced the lines of it lightly, moving onto her knees to peer over

Millie's shoulder to see where it went. Vines wrapped around her ribs and onto her shoulder blade. Then Eliza traced the opposite way, watching Millie's stomach muscles tense as her fingers danced across her skin.

"You're gorgeous," Eliza whispered, looking up to meet Millie's eyes.

Something about Millie's expression caught Eliza by surprise. There was a softness in Millie's face she couldn't quite translate. Her green eyes were wide and seemed a little guarded but vulnerable. Eliza leaned in, kissing the corner of Millie's mouth, then her lips. They kissed, less intense than before, a gentleness replacing the hunger they'd just experienced. Then Millie pulled away and wrapped her arms around Eliza's back and for a long moment they sat, quiet and still in the darkness. This wasn't what Eliza had imagined when they'd finally made their way upstairs and into bed but she welcomed it.

Eliza looked around the small studio and took in what made it so distinctly Millie. It was minimally decorated, beautiful but not packed with knick knacks. What stood out to her was a large painting hanging on the wall near the bed. It was abstract, painted in greens and browns, swirls of color on the canvas that all seemed somehow melancholy. "I like that painting," she said softly.

Millie turned and looked at it, her cheek pressed against Eliza's sternum. "Thank you. I... I painted it."

Pulling back, Eliza looked at her in surprise. "You did?"

Millie smiled, her eyes still on the painting. "Yeah. I am the great Millie Raine."

Eliza bit her lip and smiled broadly. "How could I forget?"

Millie rolled her eyes, but Eliza saw another shy smile break out on her face as she did. "You're awfully generous with the compliments," Millie replied as she put the paintings back into her closet. "Is this your preferred method of seduction?"

Eliza stretched out. "Maybe. Is it working?"

Millie smirked. "Probably." She tugged her jeans off, leaving them on the floor by her closet, before walking towards the bed and laying down next to Millie. She propped herself up on her elbow, leaning her head against her hand. The other rested on Eliza's thigh lightly.

"Mhm," Millie hummed. "I hope we'll still have time to paint, Eliza." Millie reached up to gently palm one of Eliza's breasts through her bra, then tugged the material down. "Maybe like this?"

Eliza opened her mouth to answer but before she could say anything, Millie leaned down and kissed her nipple, letting her tongue dart out from between her lips to swirl around it. Eliza whimpered, one hand moving up Millie's spine and into her hair. Millie leaned against Eliza's side, draping a long leg over Eliza's, then dragged her hand between Eliza's breasts and around her side.

She gently pressed her palm against Eliza's back, pulling her close. Eliza rolled towards Millie and she felt Millie deftly unhook her bra, pulling it from her arms and tossed it somewhere behind her.

Eliza wanted Millie, desperately needed to taste her. Eliza hooked her knee over Millie's hip, then rolled her onto her back. Millie's eyes widened with surprise, then fluttered closed as Eliza thumbed her nipple. Bracing one hand on the bed, Eliza dipped down, replacing her thumb with her mouth.

Millie made a noise in the back of her throat, somewhere between a whimper and a whine, and Eliza smiled. She grazed Millie's nipple with her teeth, then licked, trailing her tongue down the side of one breast and up the other. She bit down softly on the swell of Millie's breast and heard a quiet intake of breath as Millie gasped. Millie's hands were in Eliza's hair then, her fingers pushing the hair tie out of her hair as they moved through the damp strands.

Eliza raised her head and Millie followed suit, looking down at her with lust filled eyes, her pupils blown wide.

"Watch me," Eliza said boldly and Millie nodded wordlessly, her lips parted and her cheeks flushed a dark red.

Eliza licked Millie's nipple, one long, lingering stroke, then kissed and nipped her way down her toned stomach and across her hip bones, keeping eye contact with Millie as she did. Millie's hips rose slightly and she gasped, her eyes almost fluttering shut. But her eyes never left Eliza's, even as Eliza slid her hands down the insides of Millie's thighs, her fingers sliding up and into her underwear. She pulled them off, tossing them behind her to be lost somewhere with the rest of their clothes. Then she kissed Millie's leg, pulling it onto her shoulder.

Dropping onto her stomach, Eliza felt Millie's fingers move onto her head once again as she kissed her way across Millie's lower abdomen, eliciting another quiet gasp and a clench of Millie's fingers in her hair. Sliding her left arm underneath Millie's other leg, she pulled it onto her shoulder as well, her hands gripping the fronts of Millie's thighs. Then Eliza ducked her head and, placing her mouth over Millie's clit, exhaled slowly, warming it with her breath.

"Oh fuck me," Millie murmured.

Eliza breathed against her clit again and felt Millie's hips rise once more, almost meeting Eliza's mouth. "I will," Eliza replied, lifting her head to see Millie watching her. "Patience is a virtue, you know."

"Fuck patience."

Eliza pulled on Millie's thighs then, pulling her closer, and licked her clit, her tongue flat against it. Millie cried out, one of her hands leaving Eliza's head to grip the sheets. Eliza did it again, reveling in the intoxicating knowledge that she was the one making Millie feel this way. She pressed her mouth against her, letting her tongue dance against Millie's clit, dipping in and out of her, devouring her as if Millie was her last meal on this godforsaken earth.

Millie squirmed, her hips rolling against Eliza's mouth, her fingers scrabbling for purchase on her head, on the bed, on anything they could find. When Eliza hit a particularly sensitive spot, she was rewarded with an unconscious tug on her short hair. Eliza groaned, her mouth still working against Millie, and she felt Millie shudder.

Seconds became hours and hours became seconds as the world fell away and all Eliza could hear was the soft pants of breath coming from Millie's open mouth. She heard Millie whispering softly from time to time in that raspy voice of hers, encouragement, guiding her to all her most sensitive places.

"There."

"More."

"Oh."

Eliza swirled her tongue slowly against Millie. Millie's back arched and she gasped loudly.

"Please, please don't stop."

Eliza gently pulled Millie's thighs towards the mattress in response, opening her legs wider for more access. She wouldn't let up until Millie begged her to, of that much, she was sure. Eliza unraveled her arm from around Millie's thigh and slid her middle finger into Millie, curling it gently as if beckoning to her as she stroked her clit with her tongue.

"Please," Millie breathed again.

Eliza hummed in response and felt Millie's hips buck. She curled her finger again, slowly stroking her from inside. Millie's head fell onto the bed, both hands clutching the sheets, then moved back to Eliza's head to urge her to continue. Eliza didn't break pace, licking, sucking, curling her finger, guiding Millie towards her orgasm. Moments later, Millie's body went tense and still, then she cried Eliza's name hoarsely, curling into herself, her legs trembling around Eliza's shoulders. Eliza continued with her ministrations, slowing slightly as she felt Millie coming back down.

Slowly, Millie's muscles loosened, one leg sliding shakily down to the mattress and she took a deep breath, her eyes still shut-in ecstasy. "Wow."

Eliza smiled and moved to lay near Millie, her own eyes falling shut. "Wow is right."

A beat or two passed and she heard Millie laugh softly. "Who knew paintings turned you on so much."

"Not me," Eliza said, joining Millie's quiet laughter.

Eventually their laughter died down as Millie continued catching her breath. Eliza rested on her side, one arm bent beneath her head, listening to the sound of the rain slowing on the roof above them. She was tired. Ecstatic but tired. In the quiet, she began to doze, her breath slowing.

Eliza felt Millie shift on the bed beside her. "No," she said quietly.

Eliza opened her eyes to see Millie sizing her up, using her fingers to focus. "No what?"

"I'd paint you like this. Mussed, blushing... peaceful."

Eliza smiled. "I think you mean well fucked."

"That too." Millie kissed Eliza on the cheek. "Do you want some water?"

Eliza nodded. "Thanks."

Millie padded softly into the kitchen. Eliza watched her quietly as she filled the cups. She was thankful Millie hadn't put on any clothes; she could fully appreciate her naked body this way. She was tall, all long limbs and tattoos, her messy black braid coming undone where it lay on her back. Eliza smiled to herself. Guess she'd just have to explore more of Millie's skin to see them all.

When Millie returned, she handed one to Eliza and drank the other in one go.

"Sex is thirsty business," she said when Eliza looked at her with a raised eyebrow.

Eliza took a healthy swallow from her own cup before setting it on the nightstand and laying back down. "You're not wrong."

She watched in surprise as Millie actually went to get her painting tools from the living room. "What?" Millie asked at her incredulous look. "It really is for school."

The Roommate

39

Table of Content

Chapter 1

As I filled out the form, I couldn't think of anything else besides her eyes watching me and peeking behind me to kiss my cheek. She was supposed to be the last stop, but now I was just feeling empty. There was no time, I looked around the apartment, I couldn't hear her voice singing through the apartment and I hated it. It was hard enough that I was about to move on with these annoying memories coming in the way.

The apartment was a nice one, and we got it when we were still in love, but I never expected the place to see the beginning and end of our relationship. It wasn't so hard for me to act okay in front of people, but whenever I was alone like this, I couldn't stop the thoughts. After loving someone for three years and living with them for a year and a half, it was bound to feel this way. The worst part was that I saw none of this coming. I expected none of this to happen, but I was slowly getting my shit back together. Slow, but progress nonetheless.

"Okay." I sighed, looking at the form I had filled and signed *Piper* at the bottom.

I was already looking for a roommate. The apartment I got as an expression of love for my girlfriend was becoming a hollow space. That and the rent which I couldn't handle on my own. There was no chance in the world I could handle paying the rent alone without permanently denting my bank. I sighed for the umpteenth time, fussing over little details that would probably only get skimmed over.

After I sent out the ad, a chill settled in my spine and I relaxed, taking in deep breaths and assuring myself that a new person suddenly moving in wouldn't be so bad. I remained on the couch, eying my laptop through the corner of my eyes and refreshing the page before finally shutting it. It wasn't possible to get a reply so fast. I picked up my phone, deciding even if I got responses, I couldn't pick a roommate alone.

"Hey, Pipe."

"How many times do I need to tell you to stop calling me that, Midge?"

The woman chuckled, not bothered by the harsh tone I regarded her with, already too used to my attitude. "Now, now. You won't call me unless you don't have a choice. So, what's up?"

"I put it up," I replied, saying it casually, even though I knew she understood how hard it was for me. "I put the room up on an ad, Midge."

"I heard you. That's a brave step, but you need it."

"That wasn't why I called, though. It's up, but if I get responses, I might need your help with interviewing the potential, uh, roommates."

"You sound so formal. It's weird, Pipe." She laughed, and I frowned again. "Don't stress over any of that. I've got you covered. Tell me whenever you decide to go on with it and I'll be there for you, okay?"

"Yeah. Thanks, Midge. I owe you one."

"Oh, you owe me lots, Pipe. Talk to you later."

With that, she hung up, and I kept staring at my phone's screen, feeling a rush of emotions settling in me as I prepared to have someone else living with me. Someone else that wouldn't be her. A necessary change I needed, but I never realized how much until I met Bianca, the new roommate.

•

For the price I put in, I wasn't so surprised at the number of responses that came in. Everyone was already so invested in it and was requesting to see the apartment. I didn't waste time with that, giving them all the same day to come by and check, deciding I'd give them my rules when they came around. I also called Midge after the developments and she sounded too much like a proud mum for me to stay on the phone too long with her. After getting things ready, I felt slightly put together, but now I wasn't so sure. I stared at the girl who was chewing her gum too loudly, already staring at my face with contempt and ridiculing me with her stare. Midge had gotten close to yelling at the first two because of the questions they asked repeatedly, but this third one was plain annoying.

Her acts were intentional, and she didn't bother hiding or pretending she had different intentions. I already kicked her out twice, but she refused to leave and I really didn't want to lift her or throw her out. The time for her appointment passed already and the fourth candidate was running late.

"If the owner of the house asks you to leave, I believe you should."

The girl turned at the unfamiliar voice and I did as well, not used to such a mix. "And who are you to tell me what to do?"

"The one who might throw you out with her arms if you're not careful."

she turned to me, her chewing slowed and her eyes squared mine. "I wasn't gonna take this shit hole, anyway. It looks terrible and I have better things to do with my time. Your little bodyguard better move out of my way."

The annoying girl walked out, and I looked at the time, then back at the lady who shut the door behind her, adjusting the backpack on her shoulders. I exhaled, turning around and mentally preparing myself for a conversation with her.

"Thank you for that," I mumbled, looking everywhere except for her face. "People can be really annoying."

"Tell me about it." She chuckled, looking around the house. "Oh, pardon me. I'm Bianca and I'm sorry for coming in so late. I had an emergency to deal with that couldn't wait."

I waved it off, not at all bothered, but hoping she would be the saving grace today. However, as I showed her around and as she responded to my jokes with one of hers, I realized I liked not only her wit but her as well. She didn't flinch at my rules, assuring me there was no man in her books and her smile was friendly. She looked like everything I ran away from. Bianca was straight, and I avoided getting attracted to straight women as much as I avoided eating fries. They were always so tempting, especially once they caught my eye.

"Is that all?" She asked, looking at me in surprise right as Midge walked in. "No other rules?"

"None," I said. "Midge, I'm done with her, but you can finish up in case you think I missed anything."

"Sure thing. You are?"

"Bianca," she replied, smiling.

"Okay. Let's look around Bianca." Midge said, sparing me a glance over her shoulder like she could see the thoughts on my mind.

I really hoped she couldn't because none of them were exactly innocent.

Chapter 2

After Bianca moved into the apartment, everything else was heightened. I noticed every action the girl took, and I undeniably wanted more with her. There was no use in denying just how attracted I was to her. My body responded every single time I bumped into her and the girl was far too sweet to understand the feelings I had toward her. Truly, there were other candidates that came around before I accepted Bianca, but none of them made me feel as comfortable as Bianca did.

Now, though, as I watched her laughing at what was playing on the TV, I knew I was in for a ride. The past weeks were almost torture, and I didn't miss out on the opportunity to flirt with her. I was almost convinced she knew how I felt each time she flirted back and looked at me with her eyes. She was practically bouncing on the couch and singing along to every song being played on the award show, making sure I was following. I nodded each time she spoke, but I was too busy staring at her lips to actually care about what was showing on the television. The few seconds she used to stare at me made me feel on fire.

"Do you understand that, Piper?" She asked, pointing at some artists as they stepped on stage. "Look! They were the ones I told you about..."

I watched her as she rambled on about the show and everything else was null in my head as I moved closer to her. The glasses in her hair reflected the lights from the TV as I stared at her. My hand grazed her cheek, capturing her attention and making her words die in her throat. She looked at me with wide eyes and I slipped my hand to the back of her neck, pulling her closer. Bianca could have stepped away if she wanted, but she glanced at my lips before her eyes met mine again. It was too much for me to handle, the pure look in her bright green eyes as she looked at me. She didn't pull out of my touch and I moved my body closer, nearly groaning at the feeling of her warm skin pressed against mine.

Her eyes fluttered shut for a second, but she opened them again, staring at me and her pupils dilated. I realized I hadn't been imagining any of it after all. She wanted this as bad as I wanted. However, I wasn't willing to take that risk. I removed my hand from her neck, clearing my throat and adjusting my body away from hers. Soon enough, my body wasn't as comfortable anymore in that spot, itchy and needing me to touch her in any way I could.

"I'm just going to get a cup of water now. Enjoy your show." I said, not turning back to face her. "I'll be heading to bed after, so have a goodnight."

I entered the kitchen, closing the door behind me and leaning against it. A sigh slipped past my lips and I cursed under my breath, wondering if I had pushed too far by trying to kiss her. The look in her eyes showed she wanted it to, but it was wrong for me to be so presumptuous still. I had no right, and I grumbled, moving away from the door and taking a bottle of water from the fridge. As I moved back to the counter, opening my bottle of water, the kitchen door opened and Bianca looked up at me, smiling.

"Uh, you need a bottle?"

She replied as she took steps toward me, looking at my hand still wrapped tightly around the bottle and back at my face.

"I'm not thirsty, Piper, but it seems you are."

Her words settled in my spine and I took more of her water, letting it slide down my throat all under her gaze. She didn't take her eyes off me and she still stared at me, standing two inches shorter than me. Her glasses were gone now and no longer in her hair. When I dropped the bottle and closed the cap, I watched as she tried to cage me against the counter with an eyebrow raised. I didn't fight it, though, letting her have the illusion she was in control. I knew what I wanted with her, but I needed her to be clear about what she wanted as well.

"What do you want, Bianca?"

She huffed, looking at me with her eyes shining. "You started something only to bolt."

"What did I start?"

Bianca took another brave step closer, standing with one leg between mine while she nearly pressed her body against mine, making me extremely conscious of that there is barely distance between us.

"You were going to kiss me, but then you bolted. Why?"

I touched her hair lightly, playing with the ringlet falling over her eyes and pushing it behind her ear. "Do you want me to?"

Rather than respond, she stood on the tip of her toes instead and pressed her lips against mine. Her moan slipped out of her lips, mixing with mine, and I never expected how good it felt. Nothing I reimagined could stomp how she actually felt against my body. Wanting to change the pace, I stopped our kiss, grinning as I flipped our positions and placed her on the counter instead, pressing my body against hers. The way her heaving breasts felt against mine was almost too perfect for me to step away, and I placed my forehead against hers.

"I want to do this repeatedly."

She tilted her head, playfulness dancing in her expression as she said her next words. "What's stopping you?"

Chapter 3

My first attempt had ended with me kissing her and nearly fingering her pussy right there on the counter, but the shrill ringtone of her phone broke us right up and we hadn't gotten back to it ever since then. The thought always annoyed me, and she was even busier with work than she was before. She was barely home any more thanks to her internship at Bloomhile's. Her job involved serving as an agent to any growing artiste, so she was put under a successful agent, serving as an assistant. It was hard to keep up with the stories she brought home with her every time she came back home. I couldn't even feel less stressed because I wanted her attention.

I was determined to make today count, though. Bianca was on a break for the next three days because of the agent leaving the country. In her absence, she wasn't obligated to go to work. As much as it annoyed Bianca that she couldn't travel with the agent, I was just happy she was here. I was waiting for her in our bedroom. She started sleeping in my bed ever since that first night, but there was little chance of me doing what I wanted with her when she was always too busy to do anything. Or too tired.

"Staying up for me, Piper?"

The scent of her jasmine-scented body wash wafted into my nose as she walked in and I looked at her, my eyes nearly bulging out when I saw her naked body.

"Why are you staring so much?"

"I... I wasn't expecting this?"

She chuckled. "Are you asking me that or telling me?"

At her question, she moved closer, lying across the bed and moving her head closer to mine. She pressed her lips against mine, kissing me and making me numb to every other thing around us. I was too focused on her body and I wanted to touch her for much longer. My hands trailed down her body, sliding between us until I pinched her nipple between my fingers. She sighed, leaning her head against my shoulder while I moved my lips into her neck, biting on the skin and nibbling on it softly. I played with the rosy bud between my fingers and kept sucking on the sensitive skin of her neck until she started trying to move away from me, her body already thrumming.

I tugged her closer, placing her on the bed properly and moving my hands between her legs. A moan escaped her lips while I groaned, feeling just how wet she was. It was a wonder that she hadn't hurried out to fuck me when she came into the room. She looked at me through her hooded eyes as I slid a finger into her pussy. She was still so tight and she clenched around my finger, looking at me and huffing out her breaths.

"More?"

She didn't answer me, rolling her hips against my finger instead and looking into my eyes. My body was already there with how she was staring at me and I added another finger into her pussy, loving the moan that slipped past her lips. She acted so tough, but once she was like this, another side of her was revealed. She panted, rocking her hips until my hand moved to her waist, holding her in place. Her eyes darted to mine, and I challenged her to move away, enjoying how she looked away. I curled my fingers inside her, slapping against the sensitive spot inside her I already discovered. Making contact with that spot made her moan so loudly as she arched off the bed, getting closer to her orgasm. As she moaned my name, I could tell that it was only a matter of time before she came all over my fingers.

Just as she was about to reach her orgasm, I stopped touching her, pulling my fingers out and taking her complaints into my mouth as I kissed her. Bianca was so close to her orgasm when I snatched it from her and I knew she wanted us to keep going, but I also had an interest. I wordlessly moved our bodies until I was lying on the bed and she was on top of me.

"Sit on my face."

The red in her cheeks spread all over her face, but she still moved to obey my commands. Bianca straddled my face, looking down at me before sitting completely. She was worried about crushing me, but all I wanted was her on my face. When I had her on my face, I was finally ready to dig into her sweet pussy and savor the taste completely. There was nothing else holding me back. I held her thighs tight, and she rocked on my face, her moans sounding almost distant with her legs planted against my ears.

I lapped at her juices, trailing my tongue through her folds and flicking back and forth at her throbbing clit. I used one hand to hold her thigh while I reached the other forward. It was no surprise when she gasped as I touched her clit with my fingers. She arched off my face, only getting held in place by my fingers. She didn't seem too happy about it.

"Piper..."

I rolled my tongue against her faster, rubbing my fingers and pressing harder on her clit. It didn't take long before she shuddered above me. I released my hold on her and I watched as she slumped to the side, squirting all over the sheets and making a major mess. My eyes only remained fixed as I moved my fingers to my pussy, soaking in the view as I rubbed at my clit.

•

Bianca squirting for the first time seemed to make her more interested in whatever we had going on. I knew she was still straight, but her involvement with me had to mean something. I asked her about it and she admitted to being curious. She has always wanted to know what it felt like to be with a girl, and my touch ignited something unexpected in her. I went shopping in an adult shop and got us some things and it was also why Bianca was panting against the wall of a building a few blocks from ours.

"Can't take it anymore?"

She gritted her teeth, the faint buzz of the vibrator reaching my ears as I got closer to her. I knew she wouldn't admit to me she was getting closer to cumming. Her legs were practically jelly with the way she was walking, like she was intoxicated in broad daylight. She had tried to pretend to be unaffected as we walked to the restaurant, but now she was too turned on. Her body was responding already and I might have *accidentally* increased the volume of vibrations coursing through her. She pinned me with a glare as she pushed past me, taking fast steps to our apartment building. Each time she stopped, I stopped with her as well, praising her and encouraging her to continue walking.

There was no need to be told just how close she was, so as we walked in, she collapsed to the floor. Bianca was breathing so heavily and I turned the vibrator off, wanting her to calm down a little.

"Why did you do that?" She rasped. "I w-was close."

I looked at her. "I know. But I don't want to stop there, do you?"

She looked at me with interest growing in her eyes before I tugged her up, directing us back into our bedroom. I lay her on the bed, watching her bounce and tug her dress over her head. She had forgone her underwear again today, and I didn't mind, digging through the items I bought and bringing out the fluffy handcuffs. Bianca eyed them as I hooked her hands to the bedboard.

"You trust me, right?"

"Yes, Piper."

"Ok, and don't forget our safe word is, Sweet."

I patted her cheek, looking at her body and placing my leg between hers while I pressed my other leg on the other side. I trailed my hand to the path between her legs and I watched as her breath hitched, her body arching. My pussy clenched further, and I reached my legs as well, touching the pulsing mound and rolling my hips lightly, rubbing my pussy against Bianca's. She moaned, her clit throbbing harder at the first contact I made, and I continued rolling my hips.

The trail of juices from our pussies was serving as enough lubricant for us to move against each other fluidly. The feeling of her clit bumping into mine so steadily was making me lose my hold, and I opened my eyes to see her arching. Bianca was fighting against the cuffs, tugging and trying to remove her hand to no avail. I loved the look of desperation on her face, so I leaned closer, rocking my hips in time with my movements, feeling so breathless. My fingers held her chin in place and I stared directly into her eyes as I picked up the pace of my hips, teasing her only to slow down.

The buildup of her orgasm crashing seemed to affect her too much because she huffed, staring at me with tears gathering in her eye. I rubbed her cheeks tenderly.

"You want to cum, Bianca?"

She nodded, and I smiled, tapping her chin with my fingers as I rolled my hips faster, going back to the pace I started earlier. Her eyes rolled into the back of her head, her toes curling while her body shuddered. Feeling her cum also triggered me as I came right behind her. I didn't stop rubbing our pussy, riding out the length of our orgasms and letting it crash through us. She gasped, taking in sharp breaths while she shook. I reached above her head, pulling the handcuffs away and removing her hands from them. I kissed the flesh, smiling at her as we basked in the scent of our juices mixing on the sheets.

Chapter 4

I felt my breath run out of my throat when I walked in and saw Bianca sitting on the couch spread eagle with her pussy facing the door. She smiled at me at my entrance and I looked down at the juice I got her and wondered what exactly led to this. It had been two weeks since she resumed again at Bloomhile's with the agent back. We have been getting to play with each other, but it was nothing compared to how those few days were and I saw she missed them just as bad.

"Welcome, Piper." She breathed, rubbing her finger on her clit. "I've been waiting for you."

I gulped, locking the door as I realized there was no way I could risk Midge barging into my apartment to see this. She smiled at me, motioning that I sat and I did, obeying every one of her commands and feeling my pussy getting wet as well. I wanted to step out of my jeans so badly, but I sat anyway, watching as she dipped her fingers into her mouth, lathering it with spit. The coated fingers were what she moved back to her clit, rubbing the nub faster and increasing the pace.

"When did you start touching yourself?" I asked, looking at her, feeling the liquid trickle into my panties. "Right after I left?"

She bit on her bottom lip and nodded. "I promised myself I wouldn't cum until you came back."

"You did well. Now squirt, and let me watch you."

My words caused her to arch off the couch, sending a direct trigger through her body and straight to her clit. Her legs were shaking as she rubbed to the side faster, creating a steady slapping sound. Eventually, her toes curled, and slapped her fingers against the twitching bud, letting herself cum. She buzzed, her body shaking as her orgasm rocked through her in waves. Under my gaze, she looked at me again, squirting and moaning loudly. She held the decorative pillows on the couch in her fist as she came harder. I watched her. The look in her eyes made me stand from my spot. I held her shuddering body against mine, letting her rock her body against me, riding out her orgasm.

Bianca eventually calmed down, looking at me with the hooded look in her eyes as she relaxed. She pulled me closer, kissing me softly and taking in the moan that slipped past my lips at her act. I was enjoying the moment to pull away, but when she did, I grunted my protest. The woman only chuckled at my act, poking my nose with her finger.

"Keep the drinks in the fridge for later." She whispered into my ear. "I still have other things for us in the room."

I gulped again, looking at her before I stepped away, scrambling into the kitchen and throwing the drinks into the fridge. When I walked out, she wasn't in her spot anymore, and I hurried into the room, feeling my body buzzing with need. It had been a while since I last felt the way I did now, but there was no going back and as I walked into the room, seeing her sprawled on the bed, I knew I was right to feel this way. Arranged on the bed was a strap-on and a lube I got for us if I was to ever fuck her ass. The past weeks had moved so fast that I couldn't explain what was happening anymore, but I was enjoying it.

"Piper?"

I didn't respond, crashing to my knees in front of her as I parted her thighs, placing my body between her legs. Her sensitive nub still glistened from her juices, and the trail between her legs was still present. The more I stared, the more I wanted to taste her on my tongue. Bianca rolled her hips in the air, her eyes meeting mine and urging me on. I pressed my lips against her pussy, drinking up her cum and lapping at it.

She rolled her hips higher, her fingers slipping into my hair and gripping it, causing me to grunt louder. I was certain that with how sensitive she was since her last orgasm, it wouldn't take her too long to reach her high again. I liked how quickly she could cum and as I held her thighs down, stopping her from shutting them against my face, she arched off the bed.

"Piper, please. More."

I hummed into her pussy, slipping my tongue through her slit and feeling her clench hard around my tongue, cumming hard. I moved my hand to her waist, holding her down as she came again, struggling to keep calm as her orgasm rolled through her for the second time. She loosened the grip she had on my hair and I moved away, standing and looking at how much of a mess she was now that I was done. I stripped, stepping out of all the restricting clothing I had on. She panted, taking in deep breaths and when Bianca looked up at me, she smiled. I shook my head at her, wearing the strap on and kissing my teeth as I adjusted the straps.

The thing I loved about this was the material that was built to rub against the clit with every movement I made. It was that exact reason I got it. I wanted to reach my high alongside Bianca.

"Fucking hell." Just lining it against her pussy caused the material to rub against my clit.

I pushed the tip of the strap-on into her pussy, watching her face as her mouth fell open in an 'o'. Her eyes remained wide open as I pushed the rest of the thick length into her. She moaned, arching off the bed and bunching the sheets in her hand. Her eyes were shut now, and I wasn't too bothered about it as I steadied a pace. My breaths were coming out in short puffs and the strap teased my clit. Each thrust I graced Bianca with was making me closer to the edge as well. Her body hummed as I moved against her and she shuddered against me, rolling her hips and meeting every thrust.

My hand moved to her thigh, and I hooked my arm under it, placing it on my shoulder and changing the angle of my thrusts completely. She gasped, but she kept her gaze fixed on mine, opening up her arms to me until I lowered my body to her. I pressed my lips against hers, unable to pull away when she swiped her tongue over my lips. I worried I was crushing her body with mine, but she paid me no mind as her tabs wrapped around my arm tighter, the grip increasing. My orgasm was closer and when our tongues met, clashing in between, I moaned into her mouth, letting her hold me tighter.

"Piper... I can't..."

I nodded, knowing what she meant because I was shuddering as well, my legs barely able to keep me upright as I reached my high. My fingers quickly moved to her clit after I coated them with my spit and I rubbed at it, triggering yet another orgasm from her. I held her body, rocking into her as the material still rubbed against my clit. When I eventually stopped thrusting, her fingers caressed my face until I looked at her face before she pressed her lips against mine, making me relax against her body completely.

I drift off to sleep, smiling thinking how this beautiful sexy woman made me completely forgot about my ex.

My First Time

61

Table of Content

<u>My First Time</u>

Chapter 1

I had no plans of stepping out of my room for the day, but hearing my mum on the phone chuckling and saying, 'we'll be there,' had me reconsidering. There was no other 'we' besides me and her, and I walked out of my room cautiously, hoping I had misheard.

"Oh, there you are, Eliana." she greeted, stars in her eyes. "Flora's niece is staying over at her house and she plans to start college soon. She's about your age, and I believe you two can be friends. Her name is Raya."

"Uh, no."

"Don't be like that. She's new in town and I'm sure she wants to know more about her college. You're my best option, Eliana."

I huffed, picking at my fingers, knowing there was no way to win against her. I didn't want to babysit another girl trying to be comfortable in the city. There were enough things on my plate already as it is, but my mum wasn't ready to listen to complaints. She shoved me back into my room and instructed me to get dressed. I looked down at my pajamas and sighed. This was so uncool.

"We're leaving soon. Hurry!"

I had half a mind to pretend I didn't hear her, but Flora was nice to me and even though I didn't want to, I had her and my mum to worry about. Reluctantly, I took off the pajamas, had a quick shower, and tugged out black shorts and a halter top. This was the most effort I could give. Anything more would be pushing it. I threw it on, finally looking in the mirror and scrunching up my nose, the freckles squeezing. I combed my hair, leaving the brown locks down, not ready to tug and pack it up. When I threw on my converse, I could only hope she was at least more willing than I was to do this.

Walking downstairs, I saw my mum beaming up at me. Rolling my eyes, I headed to the door first and walked out. She locked the door, cross-checking, before finally walking ahead to Flora's house. It was easy considering we were neighbors. Still, it made me wonder why mum was always in a hurry for us to get there when it would take barely one minute to get there. She knocked on the door and I looked at my shoes, wanting to remove myself from the situation. The door was pulled open and the person standing there was nothing like Flora.

She had a shaved side, and she gathered the rest of her hair in a ponytail. The ginger hair looked unreal, and I didn't know I was staring until mum elbowed me.

"Eliana. Come on, say hi."

I blushed, noting she was looking at me as well. "Hello. I'm Eliana."

"Nice to meet you. My aunt didn't tell me she was expecting guests, but you're chill. You can come in." The girl, Raya, said as she opened the door to us. "I'll get her down in a second."

My eyes followed her movements as she went upstairs before I scolded myself, keeping them screwed to the floor. Come on, did I already forget why I disagreed? Hot girl or not, she was fresh around here, and being a local wouldn't help me. I didn't *need* her to grow dependent on me. Yet I couldn't help the way my body was reacting to her. Images of us in sexual positions barged into my mind, and I struggled to push them out, failing.

"Claire, Eliana!" Flora greeted as she came down the stairs, while Raya trailed behind her with an eye roll. "So nice to see you."

"You saw me yesterday." Mum teased, hugging her with just as much enthusiasm despite her words.

"It's Eliana I almost never see. You're always cooped up in your room."

I smiled at her words. "Hello, Flora. I hope you're well."

She replied before pushing her niece toward me. The two of us looked at each other awkwardly, but I knew it was more from me than her. She didn't mind my presence, but she also wasn't trying to start anything. I looked at her just as the wind blew past and caused her ponytail to sway ever slightly. I gulped at the sight and looked away, feeling confused yet again at the suddenness of everything I was feeling. It was making little to no sense to me. Why was I suddenly attracted to the one I was babysitting? Well, no part of her said baby.

"I don't want to impose, but I can get the vibe that you really don't want to help me with this. It's okay. I can just tell my aunt not to bother you." She said, her voice soothing against my ears.

Suddenly, I didn't want her to leave or tell her aunt anything. As much as I didn't want to get stuck dealing with her the whole time she was here.

"It's nothing. Let's take a walk."

She beamed at me, dusting her shorts and tying her boots. Her body looked nothing like mine and my gaze dropped to her tits showing in her tank top before I scolded myself, looking away. Staring was doing little to help my situation. Now I didn't want to do anything like that. Maybe if I just helped her and got away from her, I would have a higher chance of escaping the bondage of taking care of her. Internally, I slapped my forehead.

I was getting distracted from my initial plan. Before I met her, I was going to be clear and firm with her. But now I wanted to be firm with her in more ways than one and none of them weren't lewd or didn't involve our pussies touching. What was wrong with me?

"Hey, Eliana." She said, getting my attention when she suddenly started walking with her front turned to me and her back turned to the walkway.

"Don't fall," I mumbled under my breath, but she only smiled.

"I can't." She replied, certain. "I wanted to say thank you for helping me. This would be a fun ride for both of us."

I shook my head at her, wondering if her words could ever sound more right than they did at that moment. Except the ride was bound to be more annoying for me.

Chapter 2

It was getting harder for me to hide how I was feeling about Raya, especially with how easily she made it to be around her. Considering I avoided her mostly the first time we met, every other time we hung out felt so different, and I wasn't imagining things. Her eyes were the prettiest and brightest I had seen in a while and though I wanted to be sure this was nothing more than a crush, the growing sensations toward her were more.

"Don't zone out on me now, Eliana. Come on." She grumbled, pressing harder on her phone while I continued on my end. "Bored already?"

"I'm not bored. Sorry, I just got distracted momentarily."

Raya didn't hesitate to stop our game and look at me. Her inquisitive stare made it impossible for me to hide under her gaze, and I was more conscious than ever when she kept looking at me. I wanted to cower, but I remained stiff while she got closer.

"I smell a secret."

At her words, I chuckled, tapping her nose and scooting away from her. Today was another one of those days we had the house to ourselves and being alone with Raya wasn't good for my well-being. My fantasies were worsening, and she didn't even know the things she was doing or how much it turned me on when she moved so close to me when she was excited. There was something about her that just hit all my spots right. She was still staring at me when I moved away from her, moving closer to me with those eyes still wide. Her fiery hair got in my line of vision and today, I appreciated how it was out of its usual ponytail.

"There's no secret, Raya. I might be the most boring person you've been friends with, so don't expect too much. I barely got the hot gist going on around. Heck, my mum is better at finding those out."

"What's wrong then? You've not been the usual since I came around." She mumbled, her fingers fiddling with her hair. "Or is it me? Are you uncomfortable having me around?"

"Absolutely not that. It's not you, really." I stuttered, my hands waving frantically.

I didn't need her to blame herself for something that was entirely on me. It wasn't her fault that I developed a crush on her and didn't have the balls to tell her just that. Scratch that, this wasn't a fucking crush anymore. Crushes were for kids and this... was something more. One I still couldn't describe or put into words accurately. She was still looking at me, expecting an answer, and I shook my head at her.

"Look, it's just pre-stress. Resumption is upon us, and I'm far from being ready to get back to that hellhole."

Raya chuckled, her hand rubbing at the shaved side of her head. "School isn't so bad."

"You probably don't even need to study too hard before grasping whatever you're taught, unlike me. I need about three weeks' gap between each lesson before I can fully wrap my head around it," I replied, being honest about my dilemma and steering the attention off me and to other matters. "It's just complicated and as much as I love what I get taught, I still feel like I'm struggling. Mum supports me enough, so I'm glad about that."

"Well, if it helps, I don't know what to expect from college. I moved here because I was desperate to be somewhere new. It isn't bad to move to another part of the world to start a new life, is it?"

I tilted my head at her. "It's quite normal, actually. The only problem is when you're unable to settle."

"Thanks to you and my aunt, being here has been so amazing and I don't regret coming one bit. Everything has made more sense these past weeks than they ever did."

The smile that tugged my lips upward startled me, but I let it show. Soon enough, I was beaming at Raya and blushing at the compliment she had carelessly given me. She scooted closer to me, resting her head on my shoulder, and I hoped she couldn't hear the fast thudding of my heart against my ribcage. She was close, too close for safety and as her warmth flooded my arm, it trailed lower, circling my lower regions and turning me on. I gulped, looking down at her and rubbing her head, stiffening when she rubbed her head further against me, looking like she enjoyed the touch I was giving her.

"When I was moving, I had to end a relationship. I ended quite several friendships because of my move, but breaking up with a lover was kind of hard. Keeping things long distance isn't always easy, and I wasn't ready to make things harder for us."

This was my call back to reality, and I could hear the hurt in her voice as she spoke of her lover. Whoever he was, he was so lucky that he got to have her in a way I never could. She was too precious, and I struggled to imagine how the breakup must have gone for both of them. Did she cry when she ended things, or was he upset she was moving?

"Uh... sorry about that. How did he take the news?"

Raya sat up, staring at me with an eyebrow raised. "He?"

"Your lover?" I asked before my brows rose. "Or was it a girl?"

"I'm a lesbian, Eliana. Didn't all this," she gestured to her appearance, starting from her hair, "tell you that?'

My throat suddenly felt clogged at her revelation. "It's not exactly right to make assumptions, you know? It's not something I do."

"I'm messing with you." Raya laughed, bumping her shoulder against mine. "But yeah, we broke up. There were no hard feelings or anything since she was also moving somewhere else for her college. It was only right we gave each other the reins to do whatever we wanted without holding each other back."

"I see."

The silence panned out between us, but it was mainly me trying to focus on the fact that she was a lesbian *and* single. Such coincidences didn't happen too often and yet, it was happening right now. She was calm beside me, tapping away at her phone while I glanced at her from the corner of my eyes. There was no part of her that didn't appeal to me. Unlike her, I wasn't an out lesbian, and surely; she needed someone who was more open about their sexuality like she was. I gulped, looking down at my fingers.

"I should get going now, but since we might not see before resumption, we should totally plan out how we'll meet, yeah?"

I remembered my little holiday with my mom to a resort and grumbled under my breath while Raya laughed at my misery. She didn't seem like she minded I would be away, and it made little sense that I wanted her to be affected by my absence. Shaking my head at my silly thoughts, meeting her waiting gaze again.

"I really wish I didn't have to go with her."

"You don't have a choice."

I knew I didn't, which was exactly why I was going. I scanned Raya's body one last time, trying to keep my staring unnoticeable and not lingering at specific parts. Like how her pink nipples puckered out of her white t-shirt. Definitely not that. I looked down at her feet and back at her face. Doing something now would change the course of our relationship completely, and I wasn't sure I was ready for that just yet. Our friendship was barely steady as it was and if I tried anything new, it was bound to sink. So, what if she was single? Raya never mentioned she was looking for another girlfriend or that she liked me. I scolded myself internally, smacking my forehead, and smiling when I looked up.

"We can just come home on a visit. Preferably during a weekend." I suggested. "It should be after we've gotten settled though and we can keep tabs on each other through texts because I'm almost certain we won't bump into each other."

"That's okay." She nodded. "A weekend back home to hang out and update Flora and Claire about how college was going for us. That's a promise on my end. I'll text you when I can come around and you should, too."

I nodded in response to her request, smiling like a teenager again and walking her to the door. Raya turned around suddenly, wrapping her hands around my neck while her breath hit my neck. I bit on my bottom lip, circling my arms around her waist and feeling lost in the moment as I touched her. This couldn't be normal, getting so aroused from a hug she gave me. When she pulled away, I forced myself not to miss her warmth or the feeling of her body pressed against mine.

"See you soon, Eliana." She said, waving as she walked back to her house.

I shut the door after she was out of sight, leaning my head against the door and feeling so pathetic for eating up how I felt. Not once had I tried flirting with her, but now I was regretting all of that. I shook my head at myself, deciding that wasn't a shelf I wanted to open up.

Chapter 3

The switch in how I felt about keeping my feelings to myself was suddenly gone. Perhaps it was the sexual frustration that held me captive back in college or Raya, who wouldn't stop video calling me whenever she wanted us to talk. It didn't help the feelings I was struggling to keep at bay and after five weeks of leaving home, we finally went back. I disagreed when she requested, we went home together. I wasn't too sure if I was ready to see her just yet and as I reached Flora's doorstep, I knocked, looking away from the entrance.

Rushed footsteps reached the door and when I looked up, I saw Raya regarding me with a wide smile of her own, which I was sure mirrored the one on my lips. She took a step closer, instantly wrapping me in her peppermint scent and letting me glimpse at her dyed hair. Within the time we spent at school, she already changed the color of her hair, dyeing it black. She called me the night after she did it, explaining how much it felt like her color.

"Well, hello to you too."

She shook her head at me, tugging my arm and pulling me into the living room. "How could you leave me to entertain the two of them all by myself?"

"Oops," I said nonchalantly, which led to her jabbing me with her elbow. "Sorry, sorry. I had a project to turn in today."

We reached the living room, and my mum and Flora greeted me. The two of them floundered around me, tugging my cheeks and pointing out that I had gotten slimmer than I was back at home. I smiled through all of their prodding, catching as Raya poked her tongue out toward me, looking almost pleased by the treatment I was getting. I shook my head at her, letting my mum and her friend check on me and ask about how school was for me. They compared our stories and forced us to eat more portions than we normally would, as though we could gain the lost weight in hours.

When they finally left us to our devices, Raya nodded upstairs, and we excused them. The way we scampered up the stairs had me feeling young again. When we reached the room, she stared at me, looking outside the window.

"That was something."

"Yeah, definitely something." I chuckled in response, moving closer to her, unable to help myself. "Are you okay?"

"I'm fine. It's just that there are some things on my mind..." she trailed off when my fingers curled around her arm and looked up at me.

"Go on." I teased, watching her pupils dilating as she stared at me. "Tell me what's on your mind, Raya."

"You're touching me."

"I shouldn't?" I asked, taking another bold step forward and pushing her against the wall. "Do you want me to stop?"

She whimpered when my hand trailed to her neck, brushing past her sensitive buds, poking out of the dress she had on. Her glassy eyes turned to meet mine, and that was it for me. I reached down instantly, pressing my lips and body against hers. Raya moaned into my mouth, reaching up to wrap her arms around my neck as she kissed me deeper. There was a fresh taste in her mouth and I wanted to explore it. I squeezed my hand around her waist, pulling away so we can catch our breath, but we barely got the chance to when she leaned up again, taking my mouth in hers and kissing me.

I pressed our bodies further against the wall and moaned when she bit on my bottom lip, tugging it into her mouth. Our kiss was everything I expected it to be, and more. The moment was far too perfect and even when we stopped kissing; she kept our foreheads pressed together, a smile on her lips as she breathed. Raya looked even prettier when she looked up at me with her dark eyes shining.

"Have you always wanted to do that to me?"

"Yeah." I replied, already out of breath and longing for more. "Have you?"

"Since the day I saw you on our doorstep, yes."

Sharing our affection made me lighter, and we moved away from each other, already better with the things we shared. I could still feel her lips pressed against mine as she led us to her bed and we sank into it. She tugged my arm until we were lying in bed and facing each other. I reached up to brush her hair back and away from her face when she scooted closer to me until we were staring deeply into each other's eyes. Joy welled up in me because I finally told her how I felt about her.

"I like you a lot, Raya."

She smiled, pink tainting her cheeks as she flushed. "I've liked you too since I saw you."

"Well, that settles everything." I joked, tugging her closer by her waist and pressing her lips against mine again, reliving the moment all over again and wishing it never ended.

Chapter 4

I barely wasted time as I closed the door behind me before throwing myself onto her couch. Times when Raya let me into her apartment, I couldn't get over just how much it seemed like her. From the decorations to the tiniest detail, like her plant set. I exhaled, pushing my body out of the shirt I had on and leaving me in my sports bra. It was only past 6, but I knew she was on her way since I texted her.

Feeling tired of the living room, I placed my shoes right at the entrance and marched into the room. Just as I plopped on the bed, sighing in relief, I heard the door opening.

"Eliana? Where are you?"

"Over here," I yelled, waiting for her to rush into her room.

She ran in like a fireball, rushing into my arms and tackling me into the bed. She laid kisses all over my face while I chuckled helplessly against her hyper frame. I moved my hands to her cheeks, pinching the fleshy sides and pulling them apart.

"Ow, ow. Stop being mean, Eliana." She pouted, getting off my body and letting me breathe. "I missed you."

"You saw me last week."

"That doesn't count. All we did was make out like teenagers and then you were off."

If I didn't know any better, I would mistake her tone for something else, but since I started messaging Raya, I learned new things about her. Like how she wanted me to start stuff mostly because she got too shy to start them. However, she had no problem taking the lead after the initial push. Same with our kiss.

"You want us to do more, baby?"

Raya flushed. "I mean... it's not like I have anything better to do."

At her cheeky smile, I shook my head, wrapping a hand behind her head and pulling her in. Tasting the strawberry on her tongue was unreal, and I tugged her closer, drawing her back on my body. She moaned into my mouth, her fingers running down my cheeks and reaching down to palm my tits. I chuckled, pulling away and looking at her. Raya looked beautiful when she was turned on. The black hair added to her feistiness and with her on my lap like this, I wanted all of it.

"Yeah?

"I want to touch you."

"Touch me, Raya."

She hummed, rolling her hips against my clothed skin and I looked down at the spot our bodies were connected, feeling my clit throbbing. The bud begged for attention and with each roll of Raya's hips, my panties rubbed against my clit. She moved her hand to my sports bra, still humping herself on me, looking damn near euphoria while she tugged it off.

"Wow," she whispered, staring at my mounds like they were her present for Christmas. "They look perfect."

Corny lines coming from her were perfect, too. I moaned, arching my back and offering them to her on a platter or something close enough. Raya took the hint with a smile, tugging her bottom lip as she bent to take my tit in her mouth. She lapped at the sensitive bud of my nipple, rolling her hips in tune and moaning around my skin. The feeling of her hot tongue rolling my nipple had me squeezing the sheets underneath us.

Her eyes met mine, and I cursed under my breath. She pulled away, flicking her tongue over my nipple before she moved back up. Her body thrummed against mine and I knew she was closing in on her orgasm. Raya moaned, still rolling her hips as she came. I felt her juices as it slipped through her underwear and onto my crotch. I looked down at the spot, feeling myself reaching my high as well when she rolled her hips one last time. My body stiffened, and I shut my eyes, trying to remain grounded and not push the still aroused woman off my lap by accident. When I relaxed, I opened my eyes to meet her teasing stare.

I ran to the kitchen to get some ice in a cup, then I lapped at the water dripping from the ice before pressing it against her throbbing clit, circling it. She writhed on the bed, her heels digging into it. I took precautionary steps already when I bound her hands to the bed and covered her eyes. And remind her that if it got too intense for her, she should use the safe word apple. From how she was taking my touch, I knew it heightened every experience for her. All I wanted to do was tease her, then maybe have a good fingering session before we cuddled, but holding back her orgasm was making me more turned on than I wished.

"Eliana ..." she drawled, rolling her hips from the absence of the coldness between her legs. "Please."

"What are you begging for, Raya?" I asked, standing beside her. "Do you want something?"

She let out a frustrated cry. "I want to cum. Please, let me cum."

I shut my eyes, feeling her words hitting my pussy directly as though she were speaking to it and not me. Her pleas were making me aroused as well, and I stared at the bowl of ice, intentionally letting them hit the bowl as I shook it. I picked one out, rolling my tongue against it before holding it between my thigh. The coolness hit her first before the ice did and Raya groaned, arching and trying to get away, but still moving forward each time I took a step back.

As I moved lower from her clit to her pussy, the ice melted faster from her warmth and the wetness dripping. I licked the ice until the sides were smooth and rubbed my finger against Raya's pussy. She took in a deep breath, heels digging into the bed in anticipation, but she choked when I slipped my fingers in with the ice between them. Raya moaned louder, her hands tugging against the restraints while she called out to me. Her body was thrumming again, and I knew it was only a matter of time before she reached her high and came all over my fingers. The anticipation was making me keep my gaze on her face. I saw the tears dripping down the sides of her cheeks as she begged me to let her cum. I curled my fingers inside her just at the spot I knew made her see stars and pressed the melting ice against it.

She wasn't just begging anymore and her body stiffened suddenly, her cries being my name on her lips, and she came, squirting all over my body. Raya wasn't one to get embarrassed over things like this, and I wasn't too.

Chapter 5

"Hey..." I whispered, tugging off the restraints that kept her bound to the bed.

Her eyes were on mine in seconds and I wiped at the tears that dribbled down her cheeks. She looked just as beautiful as she normally did, even at that moment, and as I hugged her body against mine, she sniffled.

"Do you want us to avoid doing that next time?"

In response, she shook her head, but I kissed my teeth, pulling her out of my arms to meet her face.

"Words, Raya."

"I liked it." She murmured. "Everything felt so different once I had the blindfolds on. Not being able to touch you annoyed me, though."

I chuckled at her words before kissing her nose. I moved lower, pressing my lips against hers and relishing in the sigh she released into my mouth. There was a hum in her body as I let her touch me, her fingers curling into my dark hair and her breasts pressing against mine. There was no need for me to see her smiling because I could feel them against my lips. I moved my hands down her sides, resting them on her hips and tugging her on my lap again. She groaned, rolling her hips and moving her hands down to tug my panties off.

My hands moved to help her, and I pulled away from her lips, stepping out of my panties completely and meeting her gaze. She kept her eyes zoned in on my naked body and she wasn't just beckoning me to her anymore. It felt like Raya needed me right by her side, and that feeling was unlike any other. I crawled back into bed with her, pressing my lips against her neck and kissing down her body. Even though she wanted to please me too, all I wanted to do today was focus on her and her body. I needed to hear all the sounds she would make if I kept touching her.

Raya moaned, her hands in my hair in an instant as I reached between her legs. The warmth had covered the initial coolness I left behind and I smiled, pressing a soft kiss against her pussy. I watched as she stared at me, her bottom lip between her teeth as she held my gaze and struggled to keep her body from moving off the bed. Whatever she did, though, mattered little to me and I kept my hands on her waist, keeping her pressed to the bed. She wasn't letting me have that though as her fingers dug into my arm. I lapped at her pussy, holding her down tight as she dug her heels into the bed.

"Eliana!"

I hummed my response into her sensitive area, loving how responsive she was to every touch I gave her. The look in her eyes was hooded, and I liked just how she was staring at me. I enjoyed the neutral, tangy taste of her pussy as she filled her moans with my name. She let me have all of it and more as she watched me. She didn't try moving her body away from me anymore. All she wanted was for me to do all of that and more, and I had no interest in stopping the treatment I was already gracing her with.

I lapped further into her pussy, curling my tongue just right and wiggling into her pussy. She moaned, letting me see just how much the action affected her. Raya wasn't looking at me anymore as I moved my tongue deeper inside her. She was simply arching off the bed, letting out sounds only she could understand, and the view made my clit throb harder. I moved one hand away from her waist, keeping the other steady as I moved away and down to my pussy. She kept her eyes shut as she neared her orgasm and I was getting off so hard at the sight of her about to cum. She let out another loud moan, her hand suddenly tugging my hair and sending a jolt to my pussy. Raya probably didn't notice how affected I was by her tugging as she pulled harder.

My eyes rolled into the back of my head as she did, and I let my tongue out of her, lapping deftly at her clit. My fingers rolled mine faster, back and forth. I was bent on bringing us both to our orgasms and as soon as she arched off the bed, squirting all over my face, I dug in, lapping all of it. I loved how she tasted on my tongue and how unrestrained she was whenever she came. She moaned as loudly as she wanted, thrashing if she could. Her body stiffened, and I watched, rubbing my clit and kissing her thigh as my orgasm washed over me.

I rolled my clit between my fingers as I tried to find my balance again, but it was all worth it when I opened my eyes to see her heavy-lidded ones staring back at me. I moved from my spot between her legs, moving closer to her body and lying beside her. My hands brushed her hands away, my face still covered in her juices as she smiled and kissed me.

Chapter 6

It all started as a dare, but I didn't mind where everything was heading. Raya didn't seem to mind as well as she smiled cheekily at me, pulling her legs apart and revealing her shaven pussy to me. I took in a deep breath, pulling my panties down as well. I was sitting across from her and she had a full view of how my body was shaking. She could also see how affected I was by our dare. The one we made barely minutes ago to masturbate to each other.

In my hand was a dildo, a curved pink one she got me and in hers was a lighter pink shade I got her. It seemed like too much of a coincidence that she requested we got sec toys for each other only fit her to bring up the dare. Sometimes it was hard to see what Raya truly wanted, but I liked when she was open about her interests.

"Start whenever you want." She mumbled under her breath, looking at me from under her lashes as she circled the dildo against her clit.

I looked down at the one in my hand and squeezed it, loving the feeling of it in my hand. I moved it down to my pussy, not hesitating to push half of the length in. There was no need for teasing when the sight I had was already getting me wet enough to fuck myself. I looked at Raya's pussy, knowing she was watching me with just as much interest. She kept teasing herself, circling it around, and letting out a sigh. I looked at myself and pushed the remaining half in, biting on my bottom lip and meeting her eyes. She was panting, her eyes darker as she stared at my face and the spot the dildo had slipped into my pussy.

My body was bursting from the sensation it was getting. Having something thicker than my fingers inside me was definitely new. I rolled my hips, trying to get the spot I knew would drive me crazy just enough. As soon as the dildo brushed against it, I shuddered, trying to move my body away, but I held back. I didn't pull out the dildo, instead; I left it in that exact position, letting it stimulate my g-spot. Then, I moved my gaze back to Raya, who already had the cock teasing her entrance. She rubbed it against her tight pussy before slipping it in. She didn't stop until she had taken it down to the hilt.

Her mouth was open in a small 'o' as she took it all in. She rolled her hips while I moved my fingers to my clit. Her eyes peeled open again, and she kept her eyes on me as I rubbed my clit. Our stares made me smile, the action causing the dildo to rub deliciously against me. I groaned, looking down at the spot and at the mess we were both making on the bed. On her end, there was a puddle gathering in the spot where her sopping wet pussy was. I didn't need to look down at mine because I knew. I could already feel it all the way down to my asshole.

She kept her eyes on me and I rubbed my clit faster, looking at her as she got comfortable, keeping her legs spread further. She moved her knees to her chest, but still kept them apart enough for me to see what was going on down there. Raya moved her hand to her tit, palming the flesh and looking at me. I groaned under my breath, feeling the spit gathering in my mouth as she moved two of her fingers into her mouth. She coated the fingers in spit before moving them back down to her tits. She tugged at the erect mounds, rolling them between her fingers as she arched on the bed and moaned.

I kept my eyes on her, teasing myself after holding back for so long. Suddenly, I wasn't interested in cumming first anymore. If it meant I would get the full view of her rubbing her tit and looking damn eatable while at it, then I didn't mind. She looked at me, her brows scrunched up in confusion when she saw that I wasn't done yet.

"Aren't y-you going to..."

Her question made me smile and even with our dare, I was tempted to move closer to her and just touch her. I shook my head at her, watching as her fingers tugged harder on her nipples. I bit on my bottom lip, fixing my gaze on the spot between her legs as she tried to shut her thighs together, already nearing her high. The look on her face couldn't hide it anymore and she looked at me, desperately trying to get me to cum first, but I held back, nodding at her. Raya moaned, losing the last bit of her control as both of her hands held on to her tits, tugging at the nipples as she came.

She rolled her hips against the dildo before pulling it out and letting the squirt out fully. Raya slapped the dildo against her clit, twitching as it triggered another mini orgasm that rocked through her instantly. My pussy had the same thoughts as hers as I suddenly felt the waves hitting me. There was no warning, and I dropped my hand from my clit, gripping the sheets while I rolled my hips against the dildo. I groaned, biting harder on my bottom lip and tasting blood while I came.

Coming back to reality felt odd, as everything was suddenly out of touch and the blur was in my eyes, no matter how much I tried to concentrate. When I finally relaxed from my high, I saw Raya looking at me with a pout.

"What is it?" I asked, clearing my throat from the rasp that was suddenly in it. "Why do you look unhappy?"

"Why didn't you cum first? Don't you want me to do whatever you want?"

The basis of the dare was that whoever came first could get the other to do whatever they wanted for the rest of the day. That didn't seem like a terrible deal if I actually had anything I needed her to do for me, but I didn't. I just wanted to see her like that, over and over. Even if I didn't ask her to, she was already giving it all to me, even without my request.

"You're already doing all I want you to do. I don't think there's anything more I need you to do for me."

She blushed, and I tossed the dildo to another side of the bed, crawling toward her and finally touching her like I wanted to all along.

I tried not to be surprised when later that night Raya demanded that I sat on her face. I wasn't the type to blush when I was asked to do something like that, but the seriousness she said it with had me thinking she had wanted to do something for me for so long. She must have wanted to give me the same treatment I always gave her, but never got the chance because I was unwilling to let her go. Now, though, I didn't have a choice but to do what she wanted.

With a blush on my cheeks, I straddled her face and sat on it, feeling the breeze from her lips meeting my skin. I moaned, unable to help myself. She smiled against my pussy before wrapping her hands around my thighs and bringing them down on her face. I didn't even realize how much I was hovering over her face until she pulled me toward her. Raya moaned as she finally felt my pussy on her tongue. She didn't mind how I rolled my hips against her face suddenly. Her moans against my skin were driving me nuts.

I held onto the bed, trying to steady myself, but she rolled her tongue deeper, lapping at my clit and rubbing on it from the front. I felt out of breath with the combination of her touches because she knew just where I was sensitive and how to toy with me. My legs shut around her face on instinct, but she held me tighter, reminding me she was just as strong as I was, maybe even more. I moaned, rolling my hips and struggling to reach my high as her tongue slipped into my pussy. I lifted my body slightly before going back on her tongue.

Soon enough, I was riding her face, but she didn't mind as she moaned into my flesh. Her hold on my body loosened slightly, but she allowed me to. I looked down at where our bodies were connected and felt her tongue rub against my sensitive spot just as her fingers rubbed my clit. My body thrummed, and I arched her holding suddenly back on my waist. Perhaps, sensing that I was close, she didn't want to let go. Moans slipped from my lips, each one louder than the last, as she lapped at my juices. She took it all in and spanked my ass when I settled.

My breaths came out in short pants and when I looked at her with my juices glistening on her lips, I knew I wanted all of it and more, and I was going to have it because we had the rest of the semester to explore each other's body

Naughty Lesbian

Table of Content

<u>Naughty Lesbian</u>

Chapter 1

Alex has had the longest day at work, and all she wanted to do was drink cheap booze and then go home to crash. That was all.

She was dressed in grey sweatpants and a black T shirt, what she usually wore under her fire station uniform, because you couldn't afford to look pretty when lives could be at risk.

The bar had been crowded when she came in, which made her just sit in the corner until the people thinned out. Now, she was able to slide up to the counter, resting her arms on the surface as she waited for the bartender to head her way.

"Excuse me," came a voice to her right. "Do you mind pushing over just a tad?"

Alex glanced to her right where a woman about her age was standing. She tried not to focus on her eyes, a shade of green Alex had never seen before. The girl flipped her long black hair back over her shoulder, giving Alex a kind smile.

"Uh, did you hear me?" she asked again, motioning towards the bar.

"Oh, uh, yeah, yeah," Alex replied, moving over to the left to allow the lady in. God, she must really be out of it tonight.

"Thanks!" the lady beamed, resting her arms on the counter just like Alex. "It's so hard to get a good place!"

"Mhm," Alex hummed, turning away from the lady and focusing on the shelves of alcohol in front of her.

The lady considered her quickly before turning away. When she was sure she wasn't looking, Alex snuck another glance at the woman next to her. Green Eyes, as Alex decided to call her, was wearing tight black jeans and a flowy, red tank top. Comfy and stylish, Alex decided, turning away once more.

The bartender made his way over to the girls, asking for their orders.

"I'll have a vodka cran, please," Green Eyes told him, smiling widely and leaning forward in a flirtatious manner. "Get my friend here one too, please."

The bartender blinked, but smiled back at her. "Sure thing, sweetheart."

"Thank you so much," Green Eyes replied, giving the bartender a small wink.

When the bartender walked away, Alex glanced at Green Eyes once more, unable to keep herself from gaping.

"You need to know how to work men to get what you want," Green Eyes mused, adjusting her top so that the neckline sat lower on her front. "And I know what men want."

"Right," Alex replied, nodding over enthusiastically. "Men, yes, they are thirsty boys."

Green Eyes laughed, light and feathery that caused Alex's heart to constrict in her chest. Too bad this girl seemed to be straight.

The bartender came back, both drinks in his hands that he placed on the counter in front of the two women. "They're on the house," he told them, grinning at Green Eyes.

"You're so sweet!" Green Eyes exclaimed, picking up her drink. "Thank you so much!"

The bartender gave her one last wide smile before moving on to the next customer, his face steadily going more red.

Green Eyes turned to Alex. "Well, enjoy your drink!"

Before she could blink, Green Eyes was gone and Alex was alone at the bar with the drink she didn't even have to order herself. Whistling to herself, Alex grabbed her drink and headed over back to her table.

"Thirsty boys, huh?" She chuckled go herself. "Like you're any better."

She'd barely started to drink when a bar tussle broke out two tables down from her, and a bottle flew past her ear. Alright, that was it. Today was not the day for bullshit.

Alex pushed the straw to the side and downed her drink in one go, letting the alcohol course through her body. Green Eyes' flirtation worked enough to get a free drink, but not enough as this drink was clearly made with the cheapest vodka on the shelf. When she was done, she slammed the glass on the table, and strolled out.

It was too early and she was still too sober to go back home now. That meant she'd have to find another bar. Great.

Luckily, the maps app showed her one that was just three blocks away.

The second bar was much smaller than the first, with a cramped dance floor in the middle of the room and the bar set up on the side. And, unlike the first bar, this one was not as crowded.

Alex found a table to claim in seconds, throwing her denim jacket over it before heading towards the bar to order. She got a glass of whiskey, and spent more time glaring at it than actually drinking, but she did eventually finish. Then she had to use the restroom.

Once more, Alex weaved through a crowd, placing her empty glass on the table, and located the bathroom at the back of the room. Wiping her hands on her sweatpants, she opened the door, pausing just before entering.

Standing in front of the bathroom sinks, adjusting her lipstick in the mirror, was none other than Green Eyes. Frozen in place, her hand still on the bathroom door, Alex stared at the girl in the mirror, feeling the heat creep up her face. When she was done applying her lipstick, Green Eyes looked up, making eye contact with Alex through her reflection, a wide grin breaking out on her face.

"Well! Fancy seeing you here!" Green Eyes exclaimed, turning around and clapping her hands together excitedly. "What are you doing here?"

"Well, I'm going to the bathroom?" Alex offered, finally stepping completely into the restroom and letting the door close behind her.

Green Eyes laughed. "I meant in this bar!"

"Same as you, I guess," Alex shrugged. "Getting rid of sobriety. We got here half an hour ago."

"So funny! I just got here ten minutes ago," Green Eyes responded, her smile so contagious, Alex couldn't help but grin in return. "What a small world."

"Yeah," Alex agreed. "What a small world."

"Well, I won't hold you up!" Green Eyes told her, placing her lipstick back in her purse. "Bye!"

"Bye," Alex repeated, stepping out of the way so the other woman could leave the restroom.

All Alex got was one last grin before the restroom door opened and she was left alone.

"Either I have the best luck ever or the worst luck ever," Alex muttered to herself, heading towards a stall and opening it.

Chapter 2

The bartender, Katlin, glanced over at Alex and her appearance. She sighed softly and started to make a drink for her new guest. "I won't pry, but part of the job description is to listen to all the sob stories that walk through here. So, if you do want to talk... I'll at least be an ear to listen."

Alex glanced down with a soft sigh. "Thanks," she whispered. She took her phone out and set it on the bar, mindlessly scrolling through her social media. Suddenly a glass was placed next to her hand.

"So. Break up?"

"Huh? Oh.. no. It's just.. I had a really bad day. It's... nothing," she sighed and took a long drink after stuffing her phone back into her pocket.

"It sure doesn't seem like nothing. Like I said, if you need an ear I'll be here". Kaitlin lightly patted Alex's hand. "I'm no stranger to inner battles."

Alex watched as Kaitlin went to serve another guest and rested her head in her hand. She did this every month, at least twice. Get off work, get as drunk as she could handle, go home and sleep.

She was snapped out of her thoughts as the music suddenly changed and people started clapping. She looked up, confused, but clapped quietly as to not look out of place.

And that's when she saw her again. Raven hair, long legs, ruby red lips, and those green eyes. She'd changed into a tight fitted red dress with a slit to her mid-thigh, finished off with black stilettos with red soles.

'Oh shit,' Alex thought. She was not looking for anything in any sort of romantic field tonight. She couldn't. 'It's the drink. It's gotta be this drink'. She down the rest of her drink and tapped on the bar, quietly telling Kaitlin she wanted another, eyes never leaving the woman walking around the room.

"Seems like your mood has shifted into a much better place," Kaitlin said, a smirk in her voice. She set Alex's drink next to her hand. "Just know, she's not drunk and she doesn't sleep around. She wants a steady relationship".

"Huh? Uh, what? I'm sorry. I'm, uh... I'm not here for that kind of thing. Just to drink my thoughts away and then I'll be out of here. Wait. You said she doesn't sleep around and wants something steady? You know her?"

Kaitlin chuckled at Alex's rambling. "She works here too, as a dancer if you couldn't tell. Her name is Selena."

Alex swallowed hard as she felt a blush creep up. Instead of going down that road with her bartender, she took a couple gulps of her new drink. Suddenly green eyes locked with her's.

'Fuck'. Alex felt like she got the wind knocked out of her. She could feel her pulse quicken as this woman started sauntering over to her.

Selena stopped in front of Alex with a smirk after noting the blush that had creeped up to the tan girl's cheeks.

"Great to see you're still here."

Alex felt Kaitlin pat her on the shoulder before walking off to clean her bar area up a bit.

'Say something. You'll catch flies with your mouth open like this'.

"Uhhh. Yeah. No fights here".

'Smooth. Real smooth, Alex'.

The corner of Selena's mouth twitched up. "I can fix that frown for you though". She stepped off to the side of Alex's seat, leaning close to Alex's ear. "If you want, that is".

Alex gripped her glass tighter, her heart pounding in her ears. 'This woman doesn't want a booty call. She's a dancer. This is her job'.

"I'm just here for drinks. Thanks though".

Selena trailed her finger along Alex's jaw. "Shame. I was hoping to at least get you to smile. Maybe you'll change your mind by time I come back around." And with a wink. She sauntered away.

Alex took another drink, trying to ignore her sudden feelings for this stranger. She wasn't paying any of the other patrons any mind. Suddenly their eyes locked again from across the room. Alex watched as she circled the room flawlessly and blatantly ignoring everyone else in the room.

'What does she want? She just met me. She's beautiful. And then there's me. She's too far out of my league. This is just her job. I'm the new person in the room so obviously she's gonna single me out'.

Alex broke eye contact long enough to pound back the rest of her drink and set the glass on the bar. She tried looking straight ahead but found her gaze looking for the green-eyed woman who was definitely going to be the death of her.

Selena came back around the side of the bar and next to Alex again. "Well? Change your mind?" Selena asked, pulling herself up to sit on the edge of the bar.

Alex rolled her eyes. "Tables are for glasses, not asses."

'What the hell is wrong with you. Do you not want to see her ever again? Wait, what? Alex, no. She's not going to want anything with you'.

Selena scoffed. "In case you forgot, I work here. And what if this is part of the routine, hm?"

"Then why me? There's plenty of others here who would kill for your attention right now".

"True. But what if I'm just... drawn to you?"

It was Alex who scoffed this time. She pulled out some cash and placed it under her glass. "It's only because I'm the fresh meat here. I'll just go so you can give anyone else some attention".

'What's with this attitude? Are you trying to get her to hate you? Maybe. I can't be feeling like this for a stranger'.

Alex got up, waved a slight goodbye to Kaitlin and Selena. "This was cool and all, but I gotta go". Suddenly she felt a hand on her wrist. As she spun around, she found herself back in the barstool with an almost hurt looking Selena directly in front of her. "Okay. I'll give you a tip and then be on my way".

As she was reaching for more cash to give to Selena, the other woman was suddenly over her and whispering in her ear, "I don't want the tip. I want you to give me this dance. And then... maybe we could grab lunch tomorrow?"

Alex could feel her hands shaking. "I.. uh..." she glanced around the room, noticing the eyes on them, "drink first?"

Selena motioned to Kaitlin for a drink for Alex. "Don't even think of paying for that. It's on me," Selena barely whispered before backing up.

Alex took her drink from Kaitlin and took a few deep drinks. "I thought you said she's not interested in anyone here?!" She all but growled at her bartender.

Kaitlin shrugged. "She's not. But you're the new one here. I've never seen her fall like this for anyone. You must have something special. Go on, finish that drink. Don't keep her waiting". And with a wink Kaitlin walked off to entertain others at the bar.

Alex locked eyes with Selena again and decided to finish her drink in a couple more gulps. She set her glass down and stood up.

'Well. Here goes... something?'

Selena winked and walked up to Alex and grabbed her by the waist, pulling her close for a dance.

Alex felt her face heat up. "Um. Uh.. I-I don't know how.. how to dance?"

Selena smiled warmly at the girl now in her arms. She quickly adjusted their positions so she could lead the dance. "Don't just stand there staring. At least try to move your feet."

"R-right." Suddenly Alex felt panic rising in her chest as she started moving with Selena in a dance, quickly looking around the room.

Selena pulled her in closer. "Hey. They're looking at me. Breathe. Let me lead this dance. Don't fight against it. I got you".

Alex closed her eyes and let Selena lead her in their dance. She felt like she was flowing through the scene. Suddenly it felt like it was just them in the room and all she could smell was the woman guiding her and the alcohol on her own breath.

Before she could regain her thoughts, the dance was done and everyone was clapping for them.

Alex just blinked and was staring up at the green eyes still in front of her. "I-I really.. uh.. need to get going. I'm-I'm sorry.. for being an ass earlier. So uh.. goodnight." She slipped from Selena's arms, her fingers lingering in her hand a little too long and made her way to the exit. She stole one glance over her shoulder to see green eyes watching her go.

As soon as she got a few buildings away from the club, she took off at a run.

'What are you doing, you idiot? Give her a dance, and say yes to lunch tomorrow. You should have just left. You don't do this feelings thing anymore.'

She ducked just inside an alley and slowly sat down, back against the wall, breathing ragged. "I can't do this again. Just one lunch. Then we'll part ways. It's the only option. I'll apologize tomorrow."

With a shaky sigh, she stood up and continued her walk home.

A block away from her apartment, a car pulled up next to her and panic filled her body. She was about to start sprinting away when she heard a familiar voice.

"If I knew you lived this way, I would have offered to take you home".

Alex spun around. "Well I'm only a block away now, I'll be fine". She knew her voice was shaking, but started back on her path home. She couldn't be falling for someone so quick... again.

Selena had already parked her car on the side of the street and quickly chased Alex down. "Hey. I'm sorry if I startled you.

Are... are we still okay for lunch tomorrow? I'd really like to... get to know you outside of a club".

Alex stopped in her tracks, hand over her mouth and sunk down against a light pole. She couldn't fight the tears any longer. She didn't want Selena to see her like this, but everything hit her all at once. Selena quietly crouched next to her and pulled her into a gentle embrace.

"How... how can you crouch like that in... those heels and dress?" Alex sniffled and wiped at her eyes.

"I guess practice. But that's not important. Come on. Let me get you home," Selena spoke softly, slowing getting Alex back to standing.

They walked the final few feet to Alex's apartment in relative silence, the only sounds being Alex's quiet sniffles and Selena's heels on the concrete. "Well, we're here. So, goodnight, Selena".

She turned to unlock her door and step inside when she felt the familiar grasp of a hand on her wrist. She didn't move but felt her shoulders slump.

"Alex please don't drink more tonight. I know how Kaitlin can get. Especially when someone comes in upset. She has a tendency to be... heavy handed with her pours".

"I'll be fine. Anyway... thanks for the company".

"Goodnight, Alex. Call me if you need.. anything." And with that, Selena slipped a piece of paper into Alex's hand and left her apartment.

Alex turned slightly, watching Selena head to her car. She let out a sigh and looked at the paper in her hand, a small smile playing at her lips. After getting inside and locking her door, Alex took out her phone and put Selena's number into it.

'hey. It's Alex. Wanted to send you a text before I passed out. Thanks again. For tonight.'

She went to her bedroom and put her phone on the charger. With a sigh she got undressed and slid under the blanket.

"What am I doing?"

It was her last question to the empty room before letting the alcohol take her off to sleep.

Chapter 3

Alex woke to the faint morning light coming through the curtains of her room. She opened an eye, glancing at the time.

'10:23. Selena never gave me a time for lunch... maybe a few more minutes of sleep'.

Plus, she didn't have to go to work this week unless there was an emergency.

She rolled over, pulling the blanket over her head.

Selena had already gotten up for the day a couple hours ago. She checked her phone while she was having a light breakfast. Her response to Alex the night before was still the last message.

'hey, Alex. I'm happy you actually texted me. I hope giving you my number wasn't too much for you'.

She sighed and locked her phone.

'She's okay. She was drunk and went to bed. But... she was really upset most of the night. I really hope she's okay. I can't believe I asked her to lunch. What the hell, Selena? You don't do this. But she's different. I can tell." Frustrated with her inner war over her feelings for Alex, she got up and headed to the shower.

She left Alex a quick text for her plans for lunch. *'I hope you're okay. If you're still down for lunch, meet me at the diner on 34th Ave at 1:30. I hope to see you there'.*

Alex was almost asleep when her phone went off, slightly startling her. With a groan she reached for her phone, just to make sure it wasn't something urgent. She saw the notification and felt her pulse quicken slightly.

new message: Selena

She sat up and read the message quickly.

"A diner? I thought she'd be the one for something more... fancy? At least she's not some prissy rich girl. Did you seriously think that of her before? No. She's too nice for that."

Rubbing her temples, she got out of bed to go to the bathroom. After washing her hands, she decided to text back.

"1:30 sounds good. See you then."

She looked herself in the face in the mirror. She couldn't go to lunch looking like she got run over by a truck. With a sigh she stripped herself of her underwear and started a shower.

As the water was heating up, she glanced over her body, noting each burn scar and incision from the surgeries to save her life. She still couldn't believe she was still alive most days. And the fact she was able to walk was a miracle in itself. With a shaky breath she stepped into the hot water.

'Maybe lunch won't be so bad after all'.

Selena had just finished putting her hair into her towel and noticed her phone blinking with a notification. A smile came to her face with hopes of who she thought it was.

'At least she's okay. Don't pry if she still seems upset. You know what happened last time. Do I text back? She said she'd be there. No. Don't come off too desperate.'

She finished drying herself off, pulled on her robe, and headed to her closet. There wasn't a need to dress too formal so she opted for a pair of dark skinny jeans, a simple white button down, and a pair of riding boots.

Noting the time, she figured she had time to watch a bit of the news. She flipped the TV on and the first headline sent a chill through her body.

The voice through the TV gave the rundown, "3 years after the terrible fire at Imperial City Bank, leaving six dead, two critically injured, and several wounded, police still don't have answers....."

She kept watching, but the words started becoming a haze. She remembered that day. It was one of the darkest days of this city. She couldn't help but feel those people were targeted and it wasn't some heist gone wrong.

Alex got out of the shower and wrapped a towel around herself. Deciding her room was too quiet, she turned on the radio to fill the silence while she got dressed.

She pulled out a pair of simple dark wash jeans and fitted black t-shirt, listening to the guy on the radio go on about the weather. As she was pulling the shirt over her head, the voice caught her attention and she stopped dead in her tracks.

"It's been 3 years to the day of the robbery gone wrong and the police still don't have answers... "

Alex stood there, staring at the radio. She didn't pay much mind to the dates anymore. She knew this particular date was coming up, just not today. Feeling the color drain from her face she let herself fall to the floor as a painful sob rocked her body. She let herself cry, the memory flooding her mind. Reaching for her phone, she had full intention of cancelling lunch with Selena, until she noticed the time along with a message from her saying.

'I'm going to get us a seat saved. See you in a few.'

Her fingers hovered over the keyboard, trembling.

'You can't afford to be completely alone today. Just go'.

'yeah... See you in a few.'

Alex pulled herself to her feet, turned the radio off, and made her way to the kitchen. Grabbing the bottle off the counter, she took a few drinks of the whiskey before pulling a pair of converse on.

"Maybe lunch will go okay."

Chapter 4

"Just you today, Miss Olive?"

"Actually, no. Someone else should be joining me today".

"Booth as usual?"

Selena smiled at the host. "Of course. And a water to get me started".

She was led to her table and took a seat facing the door. She pulled out her phone, noting it was already 1:30. Her water was brought to her and she took a drink.

'just noticed the time. Hope you're okay'

Putting her phone down, Selena looked out the window. There was an unsettling feeling in the pit of her stomach. Her phone chimed, startling her.

It was from her best friend.

new message: Jane.

'Hope your date goes well! You know I'm going to want to hear about it'

'If she even shows..'

'you got it'

The door opened and a familiar voice caught her attention. "Selena said she got us a table?"

"Of course! Right this way".

Selena looked up to see Alex standing next to the table. She looked amazing, but something in her eyes was off. Worse than last night in the club.

"Sorry I'm late. Something... came up. I hope you weren't waiting too long".

"Not at all. Have a seat, please".

Alex shifted her weight uncomfortably, glancing at the door. "I, uh... don't want to be rude. Or even ask this of you," she rubbed the back of her neck. "But can I sit.. facing the door? It's just.. it's a thing I have. You don't have to".

Selena tried to send a warm smile her way, standing. "It's perfectly fine. I don't want you to be uncomfortable, especially since me asking you out was probably already uncomfortable for you."

"Th-thanks. I appreciate it." Her and Selena took their seats, just as the waiter came to the table.

"Good afternoon, ladies. I'm Kai and I'll be taking care of you. Would you like a refill of your water, Miss Olive? And what would you like to drink?"

Selena gestured for Alex to go first. "I'll just have a sweet tea, thanks".

"I'll take the refill when you come back. Thank you".

As Kai walked off, Alex turned to Selena. "Hold up. You're Olive? Like. Vine Industries Olive?"

Selena sighed. "Yes. My father owned the company. It's a long story for another time".

'Well, the cat's out of the bag now...'

"Huh. My family has done business with you guys. Didn't know the daughter of the company would bother dancing at clubs," Alex said with a smirk.

"It's... just a side thing. Gets me out of the office on Friday nights."

"So, you're still involved with the company?" Alex seemed interested.

"I took it over from my dad, okay? I'm sure you heard what happened to him". Selena frowned at the table.

Alex leaned back in her seat, hands up in front of her. "Hey. I'm sorry. I honestly didn't know. You... you're nothing like your father. You're honest and kind and so many other things".

'Incredibly hot being right up there with the kindness. Wait. What?'

Feeling a blush creep to her cheeks, Selena desperately wanted to change the subject. "Enough about me. I want to get to know you. That's why I wanted you to meet me here after all".

"Right. Um. I'm from the India, even though I don't look it, my first year in the city was rough, got into some trouble, found my way into the MMA team here, got seriously... injured but that was a few years ago now. Not much else to know".

Selena let out a soft chuckle. "While it is nice to know all of that, I want to get to know you. Not... just about you".

"W-what? Well.. uhh.. I don't think-"

"Sorry to interrupt, ladies. The usual meal for you, Miss Olive?" Kai asked, setting Alex's tea down.

"That would be great".

"And for you?"

"I'll just take... um... the House Club. Thanks".

"Perfect. I'll get that right in for you two".

Alex sighed as Kai walked off, then took a drink of her tea. "Listen, Selena, I don't think you'd really want to get to know me like you think you do. I'm kinda a bit of a disaster. And today of all days. I'm just not sure. There's a lot going on and- "

"Alex. Hush. Today is a rough day for so many in this city. If you want to talk ab- "

"No!" Alex realized just how loud she had gotten as soon as the word left her mouth and looked down at the table. "Please. Selena. No... at least not here. I-I can't".

Selena placed her hand over Alex's fist, softly rubbing her knuckles. "I'm sorry. I wasn't aware of how close to you that.. day was".

"You have no idea," Alex managed before her voice broke. She cleared her throat and took a deep breath. "Uh.. listen. Can we get off this topic for now?"

'Preferably forever..'

Selena pulled her hand back. "Of course. Um.. tell me about where you're from. In India".

Alex looked up and met green eyes. A small smile crept to her face. "Well... to start it's hot there. But everyone tries to be friendly to each other, it's like a huge extended family. Maybe that's only because I'm a chief's daughter..."

'Ohhhh I've said too much. Damn it, Alex'.

"A chief's daughter, huh?" There was a playful tone in Selena's voice. "Sounds like we both inherited something big".

Alex let out an airy laugh. "Something like that, I guess".

Their food came and they both ate in mostly silence. Selena couldn't take her eyes off the blue ones in front of her, though there was something brewing deep within them.

'She's so broken down. Holding so many secrets.. something is slowly eating her alive...'

"So... what do you do when you're not being a big CEO and dancer?" The voice pulled her out of her thoughts of worry for the girl.

"Oh.. nothing too crazy. I tinker with things in my workshop. Cars, motorcycles, things like that".

"And you're a mechanic? Man, you're pretty perfect...ly rounded. I mean.. so many pieces of who you are. Not just one thing you're focused on. It's admirable..."

'Okay you can shut up now. You're just rambling'.

Selena let out a soft laugh, covering her face with a hand to try to cover the blush that most definitely reached her cheeks. 'Oh, she's adorable when she gets flustered and rambles on. Woah. Slow down. This could easily be a last date with this wonderful woman'.

"I doubt it's rare to find someone with other interests outside of one thing. Like yourself?"

"Me? Nah. I work out, put fires out, and fight. That's about it".

Selena leaned forward, arms resting on the table. "You and I both know there's more to you than that".

Kai had quietly placed the check on the table and walked off. Both girls reached for it, Alex's hand landing on Selena's.

"Let me. I asked you for the date. It's the least I can do".

"I mean.. We can split it?"

"Absolutely not," Selena said with a wink and pulled her hand with the check from under Alex's. She took out her card and gave it to Kai as he passed by.

Alex pulled her phone out just after she felt it vibrate.

new message: Dad

Hey sweetie. Your mom and I wanted to make sure you're doing okay today. You can always call if you need someone to talk to. Love ya, kid'

She let out a soft sigh and had a soft smile.

'thanks, dad. I'm okay. Trying to not think of it. Love you guys'

"Already have another date lined up?"

Alex whipped her head up to meet green eyes. "What?! No! It was just my dad. He just wanted to check on me today. He gets worried sometimes, ya know? Living so far away..."

Selena let out a laugh as Kai brought her card back with a receipt. "I'm just kidding. Come on, let's get going".

The two walked out of the diner and started down the street in silence. Alex opened her mouth as if she was going to say something but decided against it, instead stuffing her hands in her pockets. Selena dared a glance over to the girl by her side.

She had really nice lips. Really nice, most likely kissable, lips. Selena willed herself to focus. Now was not the time to be horny.

Chapter 5

"How on earth are you tired? We just ate?" Selena asked in shock as Alex led her straight to the bedroom of her apartment.

"Who ever said anything about sleeping?" She stood with a wink, opening the door to the bedroom.

Selena felt her face grow warm. "O-oh. Well, in that case, who am I to refuse?"

First base was apparently a date, second base was skirting around your trauma, and third base was sex. Selena definitely wasn't complaining.

"Unless.. you don't want to. It's your call".

Selena laid down, pulling this beautiful stranger down on top of her. "Well.. try to get me in the mood then. If you can't.. I'll let you know," she said winking.

"Oh, I'll have you begging, baby," she breathed before kissing her.

Selena moaned softly into her mouth. She enjoyed this side of Alex a little more than she'd admit to anyone. The gentle roughness she seemed capable of when in this specific kind of mood made Selena's mind go blank, feeling nothing but hot desire and pleasure run through her body. This was the one way she enjoyed being on the bottom.

Alex bit at her lip and slowly made her way down her neck. She stopped and dug her teeth into the crook of her neck while, quite literally, ripping her shirt off.

'Well that's new... good thing I didn't care about that shirt much'.

Her hands were hot as she gently trailed her hands along Selena's sides and just under her breasts. Arching her back into Alex's touch, she let out a gasp when she felt Alex's leg between her own. Her mind started to let the desire take hold, realizing she was suddenly very much in the mood.

Biting down into Selena's collar bone, her hand found a breast and rolled her nipple between her fingers. She felt hands run down her back, grabbing at her shirt and slowly tugging it over her head. Selena noticed she was already without her sports bra and gave her a soft moan to the way she rolled her hips. She wasn't going to beg. Not yet.

She had a feeling she wasn't supposed to tease back. So as much as she wanted Alex to feel the pleasure she was receiving, she kept her hands off, opting to drag her nails down the muscular back of this muscular goddess. It suited her just fine honestly.

Alex let out a noise somewhere between a groan and a growl and she used her teeth to lightly tug on Selena's nipple, earning a buck of her hips against her thigh. Continuing down, she left love bites along her stomach and a particularly dark one on her ribs. She hooked her fingers into the top Selena's pants, pulling them off slowly while biting down on her hip.

She trailed her lips back up, stopping briefly to flick her tongue over a nipple. Selena arched her back, pressing her hips into Alex's leg. She wasn't going to beg. Not yet.

Alex reached around Selena's lower back, roughly bringing their hips together. She let out a gasp of pleasure and pain as Alex bit down on the nipple she was previously attending to tenderly.

All this so we don't talk about her trauma- ohhhh fuck'.

Alex had drug her teeth along the nipple in her mouth before gently nibbling on the on the top of Selena's ear.

"K-Alex.." she moved her hips, trying for friction, but Alex's grip was too strong to allow for too much movement. She was starting to ache with need.

"What's that, baby?" She was whispering in her in ear. "What do you want?" She pressed her leg tighter between the woman's legs.

She wasn't going to beg. She wasn't going to cave just yet. So instead of completely giving in, she let a drawn-out moan leave her lips.

Pressing their bodies together, Alex kissed her deeply, more teeth and anything else. She slowly moved off Selena, receiving a whimper of protest, and slid her pants and underwear off. Her eyes trailed over Selena, a smirk forming when she noticed her panties were soaked.

"Babe.. enough of the standing and smiling... come back". Her voice was more pleading than she had hoped.

She crawled back onto bed, gently easing Selena's legs wider. "What's wrong? Is it starting to hurt?" She pressed her tongue flat against the wet spot on her panties, humming softly.

Sucking in a breath, she bucked her hips into Alex's mouth. She knew that wasn't supposed to happen as soon as Alex pressed her hips into the bed, stilling her movement. Fighting against her hands when she felt Alex gently bite down on her clit, she felt her mouth move away.

"Hmmm. You gotta ask nicely," Alex's voice was teasing, yet still laced with her own desire. Painstakingly slow, she pulled Selena's panties off and tossed them to the floor before lightly trailing her hands up the inside of her thighs.

'Don't beg'. Selena tried to repeat over and over to herself.

"You want this bad, don't you?" She whispered, slowly running her thumb across her dripping folds.

Selena gripped the sheets, trying to force her hips to remain still. Her mind went blank, only able to focus on the thumb slowly toying with her lower lips.

Pressing her head into the pillow, she let out a long, almost frustrated moan.

"Alex.. p-please.."

The hand between her legs was suddenly missing, replaced with muscled thighs pressed to the backs of her own. Opening her eyes, she found herself staring into lust and love filled blues. "Please what, darling?"

"I-I need you".

"You have me. For as long as you want me". She placed a gentle kiss to Selena's lips.

"God, Alex.." she groaned, raising her hips to press herself against Alex's lower stomach.

Alex pressed her own hips down roughly, earning a gasp from her. "Again, please what, Miss Olive?" A warm hand slowly started trailing down Selena's stomach.

'Don't beg. Don't beg. Don't-'

She wrapped her arms around Alex's shoulders, pulling her close. "Please... p-please fuck me".

"Good girl," Alex whispered into her ear, slowly sliding two fingers in to the knuckle without resistance. She started a slow pace, rolling her hips into the back of her hand as Selena locked her legs around her.

Moaning into Alex's ear, she started bucking her hips quicker into her hand. Alex's fingers and hips continued at the slow pace. "Use your words".

"F-faster.."

More than happy to oblige, she matched her pace with the woman under her, hooking her fingers slightly. She moaned against Selena's neck as she adjusted slightly to be able to rub her own clit against the back of her hand.

Feeling Selena rake her nails down her back, she slipped a third finger in and hooked them roughly into her front wall with a hard buck of her hips. She continued the quick and rough pace as Selena whispered her name between moans and gasps of pleasure. Feeling the wave of bliss about to crash over her, she slightly quickened the pace of her fingers to match her hips. A couple rolls of her hips, and her body tensed while her legs trembled with a silent scream and Selena's name barely a whisper. She slid her fingers out, feeling Selena was close to her edge and received a whimper.

"Alex! Wha-" she was silenced with a kiss.

"Relax, babe. I'm not finished with you yet". She began trailing kisses down her stomach. She nipped at the inside of her thigh as Selena slightly wiggled her hips.

As soon as Alex's mouth closed around her clit, she knew she wasn't going to last much longer. She fisted her hands in Alex's hair, pulling her impossibly closer as she felt all three fingers return inside her. Feeling Alex's tongue press against her clit in a slow lick, she bucked her hips, crying out as she came back down on hooked fingers.

Alex hummed against her clit, quickening the flick and circles of her tongue. She gave her fingers a few quick and hard flutters against Selena's front wall. Pressing her tongue flat against her clit she felt Selena's walls clamp down as she fell over the edge with a loud moan. She didn't stop there, continuing to thrust her fingers quickly with a last second hook each time.

Holding Selena's leg open with her free hand, she gently sucked on her now extremely sensitive clit, keeping the pace of her fingers. She felt Selena tense and suddenly sit up with a scream, nails digging into her scalp as another powerful orgasm tore through her. Alex finally let go of her clit and rested her head on a shaking thigh, slowing her fingers to help her ride out the waves.

She looked up at the gorgeous stranger in her bed, with a smile as she removed her fingers, licking them clean before wiping her mouth and chin. She felt better than she had all week.

"How'd you like that, hm?"

Selena fell back to the bed, trying to slow her breathing when Alex crawled up beside her, wrapping her in her arms.

"I think I like it too much actually," she whispered between breaths.

"You, okay?" Her voice held concern, not knowing if it was too much.

"I'm more than okay, Alex. I know you didn't say anything about sleeping... but I could at least use a nap now". She cuddled closer into Alex's arms.

"Sure thing, babe". She traced random patters over Selena's back as she fell asleep in her arms. Moments later, Alex felt herself drift off with a content sigh.

College Heat

Table of Content

Chapter 1

I woke up this morning to the sound of my alarm blaring. It was 5:00 a.m., and I had to be at the gym in half an hour. As I dragged myself out of bed, I couldn't help but wonder why I was doing this. Why was I waking up before the sun every day to sweat and strain and push myself to the limit? Why was I dedicating my life to a game? The answer was simple: I wanted to be the best. For someone, me, who has never been big on discipline, I find it weird and surprising that I have to do all of these because of my passion. Things we do for what we love and cherish.

From the time I was a kid, I had dreamed of playing professionally, of hearing my name called out over the loudspeaker as I charged onto the field. I had worked hard, day in and day out, to make that dream a reality.

I love football. It's been my passion for as long as I can remember. And now that I'm in college, I have the opportunity to make it my career. I take that responsibility seriously. I know that if I want to be the best, I have to put in the work.

It's not just about physical strength, although that's important. It's about mental toughness too. Football is a game of strategy, and I'm always thinking about how I can outsmart my opponents. I watch films, study my playbook, and analyse my own performance to find areas for improvement.

But at the end of the day, what really sets me apart is my competitive spirit. I hate to lose. I hate it more than anything. And that's what drives me. Every time I step onto the field, I'm not just playing for myself; I'm playing for my team. We have a bond that goes beyond words. We know that we can count on each other, no matter what.

I remember one game in particular where we were down by two touchdowns at halftime. It would have been easy to give up and accept defeat. But that's not who we are. We rallied together, and I led the charge. We scored three touchdowns in the second half and won the game by a single point. That feeling of victory—of overcoming the odds—is what makes all the hard work worth it.

You might be wondering how my love and passion for football had come to be.

***

I woke up early on game day, feeling a mixture of excitement and nerves. I had been training for this moment all season, and I was determined to make it count.

As I stepped onto the field, I could feel the adrenaline pumping through my veins. I scanned the crowd, searching for my family and friends who had come to cheer me on.

The whistle blew, and the game began. I took my position on the field and watched as the ball was kicked toward me. With lightning-fast reflexes, I caught the ball and began sprinting down the field.

As I ran, I could feel the wind in my hair and the rush of adrenaline in my veins. The opposing team tried to stop me, but I was too fast and too skilled. I weaved in and out of their defense, dodging tackles and faking out the goalie.

Finally, I saw my chance. I kicked the ball with all my might, and it soared through the air, heading straight for the goal. The crowd erupted in cheers as the ball hit the back of the net, and I felt a surge of pride and joy.

Throughout the game, I continued to show off my football prowess. I scored goal after goal, and my teammates rallied around me, inspired by my determination and skill. By the end of the game, we had won by a landslide, and I knew that I had played a crucial role in our victory.

As I walked off the field, sweaty and exhausted but elated, I knew that I had found my calling. Football wasn't just a game to me—it was my passion, my purpose, and my ticket to a bright future as a professional athlete. And I was more determined than ever to keep working hard, honing my skills, and becoming the best football player I could be.

*****

I had become one of the top players on my college team, with a shot at being drafted by the pros. On several occasion, I'd even represented my college in interschool football games. Trust me to bring the cup home to my college. This made me popular and as expected I attracted a lot of girls. Although it felt good to have girls drooling over me, I still tried to maintain my focus because my goals are very important to me and tops my priority.

My fellow students and close friends would taunt me on how I always let "beautiful moments" go past me. "Dude, grab this cookie," one of them would always tease. But it isn't just m thing. Aside from that, I was the "life of it; of the party."

But there was one thing standing in my way: classical literature.

I had never been much of a reader, and the idea of studying ancient texts in a language I barely understood was daunting. But it was a required course, and I knew that if I wanted to keep my grades up and maintain my eligibility for the team, I had to pass. So, I showed up to class every day, took diligent notes, and spent hours in the library trying to decipher the material. For a literature text that'd take others a maximum of two hours to understand, it took me days to get a hinge of it, it was that bad. I knew how hard I tried just to keep abreast with the course. It felt like I was floating. On some days I felt totally lost. I always gave my best shot. But no matter how hard I tried, I just couldn't seem to grasp it. The stories were dense and complex, filled with archaic language and convoluted plotlines.

The class was taught by Professor Smith, a woman who seemed to know everything there was to know about the subject. She was passionate about the material, and her enthusiasm was infectious. But it didn't make the material any easier to understand. Professor Smith wasn't just smart, she was beautiful. Elegance wouldn't be able to describe her beauty. She was average in height, light-skinned; she had full hair that is known of the Western women. She had voluptuous mammary glands so conspicuous that her shirts couldn't hide them. Her rounded butts were heavy and to die for. Her thick thighs. Damn! Guys in class always drooled at her. She was an epitome of beauty.

Chapter 2

Professor Smith still kept lecturing us. Aside from learning, another thing that kept me glued to her classes was her beauty. She's always been an epitome of beauty. However, this time around, it felt like my mind was playing tricks on me. No matter how much I tried to just concentrate on her lips for the words she pronounced, I ended up seeing how succulent and luscious they were. And her heavy bosom? I loved it when she heaved a sigh and they jiggle. However, I tried as much as I can to take my mind of the vanities and concentrate.

I found myself struggling to keep up, falling behind on assignments, and worrying that my grade would suffer. It was a stressful time, and I felt like I was constantly on edge. But as the weeks went by, I started to notice something about Professor Smith. Something that made me want to go to her office hours, not just for help with my assignments but to spend more time with her.

It started with little things. I would catch myself stealing glances at her round boobs during class, admiring the way she spoke with such authority and grace. I loved how her lips moved when she spoke. She had total control of the shapes they took when she pronounced words. For a class that I didn't like and dreaded, I found myself looking forward to her lectures, even though they often left me feeling confused and frustrated. And when I saw her around campus, I felt a jolt of excitement in my chest – like a young school boy who'd just seen his crush.

I always had my eyes fixated on her body whenever she was walking. Gracious God! Such a beautiful work of art. Her beautiful skin radiated under the sun. I really wanted to approach her and tell her how mesmerizing her beauty was. But she is my lecturer and I don't have such gut. I continued watching her from afar and in class.

It wasn't until one particularly difficult day that I finally worked up the courage to approach her after class. I was feeling defeated and helpless, struggling to understand a passage from The Odyssey that seemed to be written in a foreign language. I must have looked like a lost puppy, because when I asked for her help, she smiled warmly and invited me to her office hours. Her smile was so warm and for a second it felt like my heart stopped beating. It was difficult to recollect myself, but I finally did.

When the time came, I walked into her office, feeling nervous and awkward. I had never been alone with a teacher before, especially not one as intelligent and beautiful as Professor Smith. But as she explained the material to me, breaking it down into smaller, more manageable pieces, I found myself feeling more relaxed. I was grateful for her patience and her kindness. I had never understood lecturer like the way I just did. "Why haven't I come to her? She doesn't even bit." I thought to myself as I left her office.

As the semester went on, I found myself visiting her office hours more and more often. It wasn't just about the material anymore; it was about her. I wanted to spend time with her, hear her thoughts on the world, and share my own with her. I found myself opening up to her in ways that I had never done before, telling her about my hopes and fears, my struggles and triumphs. She was very understanding to my plights. She was so smart that she had the right answer to every question and solution to every problem. How can a woman be so beautiful yet smart? I enjoyed our sessions together and I always looked forward to meeting her. I went to her office during break hours and after lecture periods.

Too bad, she didn't know the effect she had on me.

On this Tuesday, after she'd finished teaching us, I'd followed her to her office for better clarification. I was lost at some point of the lecture when I got carried away by her hips as the swayed as she walked around. She offered me a seat opposite hers –my favourite position. From here I can visualize every part of her perfectly.

She was arranging the files on her table when her pen fell to the floor. She bent over to pick it up and like a flash I saw the full mounds on her chest. The literary soiled from her shirt. I couldn't take my eyes of them. I was lost as I stared at them without knowing she was staring back at me. I was jolted back to reality when she cleared her throat.

I was dead embarrassed and scared that she'd be mad at me for staring at her lustfully. But, to my greatest surprise she smiled at me. It kind of gave me some relieve and I relaxed back into the chair that I was sitting on.

"You have the most beautiful body that I've ever seen." I said, surprised at my words. She blushed and said "thank you". That was the sexiest "thank you" that I've ever heard all my life. The sound of it gave me this tingly sensation and I could feel the adrenaline surge through my system. She was not just sexy, she was sweet.

I ran my eyes all over her body as I licked my lips. She continued blushing. I loved that I had such effect on her.

Chapter 3

I woke up feeling pretty exhausted this morning. It's a Saturday morning. It's been a tedious week at school. However, unlike other weeks and semesters, there is something interesting about the stress recently that makes me look forward to it. It felt so good that I totally want to be submerged in it. Don't look at me that way. If you were in my position, you'd do same.

Still in bed, I started thinking about Professor Smith again; such a beautiful angel. The thought of her succulent boobs mesmerized my thought and in no time, my dick was hard as a rock. It was so hard that it felt like it'd rip my brief. I held my shaft and stroked it. I imagined what it'd feel like to have her luscious mounds in my hands, fondling and tilting her nipples. What her lips would taste like. She has an angelic voice when she spoke. Oh! How sweet the melodies of her moan would sound in my ears. I imagined grabbing her voluptuous buttocks and smacking them at intervals. I continued stroking my hard shaft. I imagined bending her over and thrusting into her wet pink pussy. How tight it'd be. I intensified the stroke on my shaft. I could almost feel her body on mind. Like a flash I nutted and spilled my cum all over my bed. I heaved a sigh of relieve, stood up and went to wash up.

I had football training by 10 AM. I had 30 minutes left to prepare.

The weekend was so fast that the new week came in a blink of an eye and I couldn't be less grateful.

We were supposed to have Professor Smith's course by 12:30 PM, as the second lesson of the day. But she never showed up. On a normal day, I'd have been glad. But not today. I was worried. After my last class, I went to her office to check on her and she wasn't on seat. I became more worried. Why hadn't I gotten her mobile number? What could be wrong with her? It's so unlike her to miss her class. I was forlorn. I went home looking defeated. This was surely not a good way to start the week. I missed her presence. I missed seeing he beautiful face and curvy body. I prayed that she was fine and would come to school the next day.

All through that night her thought filled my mind. I tossed back and forth on the bed. I even dreamt of her.

I found it strange. The thought of her has eaten so deep into my subconsciousness that I now dreamt of her. Amazing! I couldn't sleep till the dawn of the next day –Tuesday. This made me to wake up later than usual. I had my first class for the day 11:30 AM. The time was 10:20 AM. I had forty minutes to prepare. It wasn't long before I was ready for school. The next bus at the station would be in 1 hour. I didn't want to be late for. So, I swiftly ordered for Uber. In no time I was at school.

I intentionally walked through Professor Smith's office –although it was a longer route to my class –to see if she was in school today.

Great news! Her office window blinds were up –that means she is around. I felt elated. I'd wanted to go in, say hello, and watch her beautiful lips arch into a wide smile. But there were some students sitting and talking with her. I was pissed. Well, not totally bad, I thought. At least she was in school; I could go back later and see her.

While classes were going on, all I thought about was her. It felt as if the time became slow and the hours longer. I badly wanted to get out of my class, run to her office and place my head on her boobs while stroking her hair. The classes almost bored me to death. I was so excited when the last class finish. I bid my friends goodbye, and off I went for professor Smith's office.

At her office, I knocked on the door. "Come in" her sweet melodious voice called out. I walked in and she was sitting on her chair, radiating with beauty. Was she looking more beautiful? Or, were my eyes playing a trick on me? I was star struck. Her shirt perfectly clung to her body like a second skin, and the brown colour complemented her light skin. Her long hair was packed in a bun and she had red lipstick smeared on her lips making them more profound and succulent –how badly I so wanted to kiss those lips.

"How are you, John?" Her soft voice drew me back to reality. "Professor Smith." I stuttered. "I am fine. How are you?" She smiled and pointed to the seat before her and asked me to make myself comfortable. When I'd asked, she told me that she'd travelled to LA for a workshop.

"I missed you" I caught myself saying. This time I was courageous enough. She smiles and said she missed me too. My heart skipped at the sound of that. She stretched her hands reaching for mine. Her touch was so soft and loving. I was almost lost in the euphoria of the moment when a knock came at the door. It was another lecturer. I stood up and excused myself while mouthing that I'd see her the next day. I cautiously walked out from her office while stealing glances at her. I was shocked to see her staring at me. I've never seen a star so sensual like hers.

Chapter 4

The semester quickly came to an end and to my greatest surprise I'd passed the one course that was giving me a hard time –Classical Literature. I was elated and marvelled beyond words. Of course, it wouldn't have been possible without the help of Professor Smith. I owe her a heartfelt appreciation, I thought.

My friends and I were hanging out, so I decided to go see Professor Smith at her office after sitting out with the boys.

3:30 PM.

I'd been with my friends and it felt like they weren't ready to go. And, it was important that I met Professor Smith. I excused myself and left for her office.

On getting to her office, I knocked. I didn't let her to respond before I quickly went in closing the door behind me. She was standing in front of her bookshelf with her ass jiggling as she stretched and tiptoed to reach for the book at the upper shelf.

She turned with her usual warm smile on her face. But this time there was something unusual about her smile that I found sensual. It also looked as if she did it on purpose. "John, you are here. How are you?" She asked. "I am good." I quickly replied.

She looked at my face as if asking, "Why are you here?"

"I saw my grade on Classical Literature. I passed. And, I thought to come say thank you. You've been nothing short of amazing to me. I couldn't have done this without your help and patience." I said while reaching out for her wrist. She didn't decline my touch.

She continued looking at me as we both stood facing each other without saying a word. I wanted to kiss her badly. But I was scared of what she'd think of me. Before I could say anything more, she drew me closer to herself and locked her lips with mine. It felt like a dream. Just that this dream is my reality.

I was too shocked at first that I didn't reciprocate her kiss. But when I got myself, I swung into action. I held her by the waist and drew her into me. She smelt like a mixture of roses and chocolate. Her skin was so soft and smooth that my hands ran seamlessly through her arm. Her lips were soft, softer than I'd imagined. And, her breath smelt of sweet mint. I loved it. We were locked in a slow passionate kiss. She took in my tongue and sucked at intervals. This sent hot sensation through my body and ticked in my brain. She kissed as good as she lectured her students. The kiss got intensified and I reached for her ass. Damn! How much I have wanted to have these beauties in my palm. I fondled them and she let out a loud moan. Her moan was a melody to my ears. She bit my lips and tightened her grip on my neck.

I reached for her shirt buttons and started undoing them and I was mesmerized by the glorious sight my eyes fell on. Her boobs were quite large and so sexy as they were cupped in the tight bra with a slight glimpse of her areola. The sight of them got me so hard I could feel the bulge threatening to ruin my pants. I started kissing her again with my right hand delicately fondling her left boobs and my left hand on her ass. While at it, I carefully walked her to the table. I hastily moved the books and papers on it with some of them falling to the ground. Who cared? I gently placed her on the table and continued fondling her boobs as I kissed her.

She took off my shirt with a soft whisper, "I want you inside me." I returned the favor by unhooking her bra, after which I buried my face in her succulent melons. She let out different pitches of moans as my mouth and hands played with her rock-hard nipples. She let out a sharp moan when I bit her nipple, and told me to do it again. I did and she moaned even louder, before freeing my bulging cock from the confinement of my pants.

"Oh My God" she exclaimed as she laid her eyes on my nine-inch dick. From the trance-like look on her face, she had never seen a cock as big as that in real life. We kept on kissing while she slowly massaged my cock, sucking my tongue more violently like she wanted to get all the saliva in my mouth. She went on her knees and tasted my precum. "It tastes so good" she said, as she put the head of my dick in her mouth. She could barely fit all the tip on her first attempt, but slowly she swallowed more inches before I felt the back of her mouth. Her mouth was so wet I could only imagine how her pussy would be. She inserted a finger in her pussy as she gobbled on my dick. I picked her up, put her on the table, removed her tongs, then put my mouth to work on her pussy. Her moans got more intense as I played with my tongue around her clitoris. Licking, sucking and biting on her genital made me even harder, and made her moans louder but I wasn't done feasting on her waters.

I inserted one finger slowly into her pussy, then two, while my mouth remained busy on her clitoris. "I'm going to cum" she said as her body trembled. I felt as the walls of her pussy tightened, but I didn't expect my face to be splashed with her squirt. I was ready to fuck. I stood up and kissed her as she laid on the table. She wrapped me with her legs, before reaching for my cock and inserting it in her pussy.

Her pussy was so tight but the wetness gave enough lubrication for my cock to slide in and out seamlessly. With every thrust my dick went deeper into her coochie. The faster my thrusts were, the louder her moans. The walls of her pussy tightened yet again, and I knew she was about to cum so I stopped thrusting. "Why did you stop?" She asked as I kissed her. "I want you to get on top." She climbed on top of the desk and slowly rode my cock. The sight of her bouncing boobs as she rode me made me even harder. I put them in my mouth as I held her waist and started thrusting. She gave out a loud shriek before squirting again. She kissed me passionately as I stood up from the desk while my dick was still inside her. As I carried her up and down my cock while standing, she let out another loud moan before her pussy contracted and pushed me out.

I put her down and she immediately started sucking my dick again. "Cum in my mouth" she said as she tasted her juices. All nine inches of my dick was in her throat now. I came so hard inside her stomach that my legs shook and I almost fell down. I sat down on her chair while she kept working her mouth on my cock as it slowly got softer.

She continued sucking my cock and in no time, it got hard again. With vigor and strength of a lion chasing its prey, I stood from the chair and bent her over with her hands placed on the desk for support. Her pussy was still wet and dripping. I slid into her tight wet pussy and started thrusting her slowly. She let out a soft moan. I reached for her dangling boobs and held them tilting her nipple. It felt so good inside her that I let out a sigh. "Harder, please. Fuck me harder, John" she said pleadingly. It felt as if her words were some manpower. It gave me more strength and I started thrusting harder and faster –her moans feeling the room. I lifted her thigh giving in room to thrust deeper. Like a flash, I felt my body jerk in vibration and I spilled my juice inside her. It felt so good.

Her breath was heavy and so was mine. I've never had sex so good. She turned to me with a smile on her face. "Let's do this again some other time, but next time at my place", she said as we put our clothes back on. I kissed her and said "can't wait."

www.ingramcontent.com/pod-product-compliance
Lightning Source LLC
Chambersburg PA
CBHW072233150726
48002CB00005B/2062